EVE DEVON

I write sexy heroes, sassy heroines & happy ever afters...
Growing up in locations like Botswana and Venezuela gave
me quite the taste for adventure and my love for romances
began when my mother shoved one into my hands in a
desperate attempt to keep me quiet during TV coverage of
the Wimbledon tennis finals!

When I wasn't consuming books by the bucketload, I could
be found pretending to be a damsel in distress or running
around solving mysteries and writing down my adventures.
As a teenager, I wrote countless episodes of TV detective
dramas so the hero and heroine would end up together every
week. As an adult, I worked in a library to conveniently
continue consuming books by the bucket load, until realising
I was destined to write contemporary romance and romantic
suspense myself.

I live in leafy Surrey in the UK, a book-devouring, slig
melodramatic, romance-writing sassy heroine with
own sexy hero husband!

La
Bowra...
Preston PR1 2UX

Lancashire
County Council

www.lancashire.gov.uk/libraries

LANC.

D1428184

30   142 5

Her Best Laid Plans

EVE DEVON

HarperImpulse an imprint of
HarperCollins*Publishers* Ltd
77–85 Fulham Palace Road
Hammersmith, London W6 8JB

www.harpercollins.co.uk

A Paperback Original 2014

First published in Great Britain in ebook format by HarperImpulse 2014

Copyright © Eve Devon 2014

Cover Images © Shutterstock.com

Eve Devon asserts the moral right to
be identified as the author of this work

A catalogue record for this book is
available from the British Library

ISBN: 9780007591626

This book is dedicated to my Husband—thank you for believing in me and for being the one I dance in the rain with and to my Mother—thank you for teaching me to love all the words and encouraging me to write from the moment I could put pen to paper.

Chapter One

Amanda Gray slipped into the busy New York street, her hand quite unwilling to relinquish its death-grip on a medicinal macchiato. Breathing in its sweet, reassuring aroma she pondered her next move. So much for her New Year's resolution—she was seriously out of practice at this whole taking-control-of-your-own-destiny caper.

The plan had been to ace the job interview, not babble excessively or give the impression that she couldn't organise her way out of a paper bag. But big-time nerves, combined with rusty interview skills, had shaken her, rendering her embarrassingly ineffectual, so that now some perfectly qualified and properly experienced personal assistant would get the position at the gallery instead of her.

Jostled from behind, she managed to save both her coffee and her natty new interview suit from an unfortunate coming together. Picking up her pace she fought valiantly against a case of serious pedestrian envy—everyone appeared to know exactly where they were going. She knew where she needed to get to... a job that paid enough for her to move out of the house she shared with her brother Mikey. It was the least that he deserved after he'd worked so hard to win back his independence after the accident. Seeing his progress and his capacity to fearlessly embrace life again had forced Amanda to take a look at her own.

So here she was. Absolutely, totally, one hundred per cent ready to kick-start her life again.

The fire-blanket of butterflies that settled in her stomach was amazingly effective at dousing any melancholy she felt over her interview. Her breath hitched. She was nearly used to the butterflies trumping any feelings of confidence in her ability to make changes in her life. But since coming up with "The Plan" she reminded herself life was now all about feeling the fear and doing it anyway.

Of course, she could always take the easy option and accept Jared's job offer. Except she was fairly sure the question she needed to be asking herself was "why" her brother's best friend had offered her a job. Things between them were—she quaffed back a healthy dose of macchiato to eliminate the lick of heat she felt rush to her cheeks—weird enough as it was. Or not, she hastily corrected. There wasn't any one thing about her and Jared King that needed to be complicated.

Stepping from the stream of traffic, she rooted around in her bag for her phone. Dragging it to the surface, she clicked on the memo function to bring up 'The Plan'. She'd written it six weeks ago at brand-spanking-ly-New-Year's-Day o'clock, boosted by several large cocktails in celebration of her brother's new job with a firm of lawyers. That Mikey had challenged the hand he'd been dealt, and secured himself a fulfilling future had filled her with pride. But celebrating Mikey's success as they welcomed in the New Year with all of their friends, it had suddenly dawned on her that if she didn't make some changes to her own life, she was going to be left behind. While everyone had started counting down the seconds, she'd started thinking.

Mikey had already spent his late teenage years practically raising her. On the cusp of starting his new life, there was no way she wanted to be responsible for holding him back. With alcohol making her brave she'd whipped out her phone and set about typing a three-point plan.

1) Get a better, more challenging, job that could turn into a career.

2) Move out into own place.

3) Do something with your photography.

The next day, faced with a familiar fear of change, she'd gone to delete her fledgling plan, only to thankfully remember that Mikey didn't deserve to start worrying that his sister was in danger of turning into a bit of a flake.

So, okay, she was a novice at changing the course of her life. And maybe the plan read a bit like a list. But for Amanda it was more of a resolution anyway. A New Year's resolution to participate in her own life story. Scary as that felt. Unsafe as that felt. *Tempting fate as that felt.* She had to try.

Now, scanning her eyes over the plan's contents it was as she'd suspected. Nowhere on her new life plan did it say anything about Jared King. Or acknowledging rushes of heat brought about by Jared King.

Her eyes flicked to the last entry: Do something with your photography. There was a reason it was at the bottom of the list, she conceded, noticing a text had come through whilst she'd been in the interview.

Pacing to keep warm she opened it and read: **CODE RED. WHERE R U? J**

The clack, clack, clacks of her heels slowed against the sidewalk even as her heart rate sped up. Jared's SOS text meant he needed help ousting his Latest Limpet back to The Real World, where it was clearly understood her time with the millionaire corporate property investor was up.

She should ignore it. Concentrate on 'The Plan' instead and fill out a few more job applications.

Still. He was a friend in need…

Sending a quick response, she hailed a cab. Destination: The Thai Lounge. Jared's preferred venue for dealing with 'Code Reds'.

Not that there were many. Mostly women knew the score and enjoyed their time with him. for what it was: a mutually enjoyable interlude. It was only occasionally a woman morphed into full-on Limpet mode.

That was where she came in. An arranged 'chance meeting' between her and Jared with some subtle flirting was usually enough to leave the impression that he had effectively moved on.

Leaning back against the cab's fading leather, Amanda admitted to a tiny, miniscule really, loss of perspective where Jared and their sporadic role-playing Limpet-dispensing exercises were concerned. Because for all that was up-front, solid, responsible and in-control about Jared—there was, lurking just beneath the surface, a hint of danger and a dark sensuousness that any woman would be inclined to want to try and entice out to play. Add in the six-feet-two, exquisitely muscled, chiselled cheek-boned, full-lipped, green-eyed, raven-haired wrapping and well...

Amanda squirmed. Darn it, was she going to have to get out "The Plan" again?

She chewed on her bottom lip. Maybe these days the camaraderie between them had been replaced with something far less easy to label—he still needed her help didn't he?

The light on Jared King's phone flashed and he shot a glance to his companion before picking it up to read his message.

'I'll be there in fifteen. You owe me ;-) Amanda xx'

He breathed out silently, though his shoulders relaxed maybe a millimetre and switched off the device before replacing it on the table. Briefly he lamented not having time to make the text more explicit, but he'd sort it out with her when she arrived.

Glancing back down at the familiar menu before him, he frowned, unable to concentrate. Of their own accord, his eyes glanced at the woman sat opposite him.

Ostensibly, she too was looking at the menu, but every time his eyes lowered he could feel her silently assessing him.

He'd tried telling himself she had to be feeling as shot-to-pieces uncomfortable as he was. But all evidence pointed to the contrary. The long flight and lengthy wait in his office must have given her all the time she needed to compose herself.

He, on the other hand, had returned from a property acquisition meeting to find his PA Janey close to carrying out a discreet security check on his very non-scheduled visitor.

That had been twenty minutes ago.

Normal state of play—twenty minutes was nineteen minutes longer than he needed to bounce back after a shock.

But then he hadn't planned to be meeting a sister he hadn't set eyes on for ten years.

He tried unobtrusively to check his watch. Surely fifteen minutes had come and gone. Where was Amanda? He needed her particular brand of easy-flow, relaxed small-talk to soothe his shock and cover the awkward silences while he figured the angles.

Instead, he sat, waiting for his sister, Nora, to speak whilst silently processing a thousand questions and their myriad answers as to why she was here.

'Aren't you even going to ask how he is?' Nora asked with the succinct and confident tone provided by years of the best education money could buy.

Without looking up from the menu, Jared, careful to absent all inflection from his words, asked, 'How is he?'

She sighed, 'Do you really want to know or are you just being polite?'

'I could tell you I really want to know but after ten years in New York maybe I'm no longer as polite.'

'Wow. I thought it would be easier than this. I must have been mad. I guess I thought when I saw you I'd be able to cut to the chase.'

Jared felt his chest tighten. 'I'd say getting on a plane, travelling thousands of miles, and coming to my office pretty much equates with cutting to the chase. How'd you know where I worked

5

anyway?'

'I asked everyone's faithful friend, Google.'

Her sarcasm slammed into him and he knew he deserved every bit of it. He hadn't exactly made himself invisible in New York, but he hadn't made it especially easy to find him either.

But then, never for one moment had he assumed any of them would want to.

He thought back to the last time he'd seen her. It had been her nineteenth birthday party. He had known then that he was leaving; his bag already stowed next to his beloved motorbike at the foot of the sprawling King estate.

Guilt worked its way up from his gut.

For want of a sense of order he did what was expected of one in a restaurant and signalled a waiter.

As soon as the waiter left, Nora leant forward. 'Look, I'm just going to come right out and say this before I totally lose my nerve. I, that is—'

Jared picked up his imported beer and drank to coat the swirling emotion he now felt in his stomach. The Kings didn't do hesitation. It was educated out of them. Decide upon what to say. Then say it. Leave no room for misinterpretation.

He watched as Nora swept her hand over her sleek black bob. Her hand was trembling. Damn it, where was Amanda?

And then Nora found her voice and Jared heard only the first sentence before the anger gathered and threatened to spew from his solar plexus like a scene out of Alien.

Locking his jaw, he breathed in, forcing himself to acknowledge the fullness of what she was saying. His eyes dropped to his sister's delicate hand resting on top of his clenched fist, offering comfort; something he wasn't entitled to—making it the last thing he wanted.

'You're sure of this?' he ground out.

She nodded and he was left reeling. Until he remembered he was a King. 'Well I can give you my answer now. It's a resounding "no".'

6

'And since when has a King ever taken "no" for an answer?'

The question hung in the air, and Jared realised that his little sister had grown up, inheriting a few of the old man's traits along the way. He breathed out slowly. 'I don't care if you take it or not. My answer won't change.'

He felt himself being assessed once more and wasn't at all comfortable it was his baby sister doing it.

'Look, I realise this must have come as a bit of a shock, but aren't you a bit old to still be cultivating the tortured, bad-boy image?'

Jared withdrew his fist from the table and stretched it out on his thigh. Image? He'd always assumed he'd sealed his reputation when he'd left, without a backwards glance for the sisters who'd once looked up to him, who'd once believed in him.

As the waiter arrived to place piping-hot dishes on the rotating glass plate at the table's centre Jared kept his expression deliberately blank.

He needed a moment to adjust, that was all.

Shock could do strange things to a person.

Something he knew for a fact when he turned his head slightly to the woman doing the siren-like slow-mo walk through the maze of tables towards him, and briefly imagined that it was Amanda.

Cataloguing sexy high heels, black pencil skirt and form-fitting black sweater, long chestnut hair and flawless creamy skin... all his thoughts lurched to a stop when he zeroed in on the pair of twinkly, button-brown eyes.

Alright. Okay. There had to be a really good explanation as to why Amanda Gray had walked in wearing something so far removed from her usual garb. He couldn't help but look at her in a thoroughly off-limits way and if he didn't stop staring in the next ten seconds, all hell was going to break loose.

Nobody blind-sided him twice in one day.

'On your way somewhere special?' he asked, inwardly cursing the gravel-like quality to his voice as he rose automatically from his chair to greet her.

She shrugged her shoulders as if it wasn't important and yet a part of him, the part which had sat up to take notice as soon as she'd entered the room, wanted to beg to differ. Shock had got a hold of him. Simple as that, he cautioned, as displacement therapy played dirty with his mind, telling him it was perfectly okay to respond to the sweet temptation of Amanda leaning into him.

He felt some of his famous constraint shake loose. Felt the devil-may-care attitude he'd stamped so forcefully from his personality ten years before resurface with a thud to beat a rhythm over his consciousness and awaken the Jared of old.

Amanda caught the watchful, sexy glint in Jared's eye and had a little wobble. From the moment she'd entered the restaurant and seen Jared's beautiful companion give what could only be described as an impassioned speech she'd suspected this particular Limpet was going to be more difficult than usual. She'd watched, mesmerised, as Jared's hand had withdrawn from the woman's and an expression of complete control had fallen across his features blotting out any trace of weakness. It had had her itching to photograph the change in him, itching to capture such a remarkable skill.

She'd seen his mask slip into place only once before, when she'd awoken in the small hospital room to find him bent over her brother's bed, desolation, guilt, anger and grief etched across his features. She must have made a sound intending to comfort because the moment he'd realised she was there, his face had suddenly turned impassive and emotionless. BAM! The shutters were down!

Now, as she leant into him in greeting and watched him watching her, the words 'playing with fire' were practically tattooed onto her brain—which was ridiculous. This was Jared; her friend Jared. This was just a game to get him out of an awkward situation. This was not the time to engage heart over head. But as Jared's hand snaked out to wrap around her waist and steady her, as she was enveloped in the solid heat of his embrace, his breath fanning against her cheek and raising a thousand skittering goose-bumps

8

over her flesh, Amanda felt compelled to dismiss the wobble, and go with her gut—bypass subtle flirting and head straight to staking a claim.

Eyes welded to his, she rose up on tiptoes and brushed her lips lightly over his.

Any remaining sense of perspective promptly vanished.

Shocked, she withdrew her lips a fraction, her eyes moving uncertainly from the fullness of his lips to check his expression. As she saw that he had closed up, she was driven, if only to salvage a little pride, to revisit his lips with the soft glide of her tongue against his lower lip.

She heard the quick hiss of his indrawn breath and she responded instantly. Every last bit of her melted as his hand plunged deftly into the ponytail at the base of her neck, anchoring her so that he could take control and deepen the kiss. His tongue stroked masterfully over and under her tongue and she clung to him; one hundred per cent complicit in becoming a banquet on which he could greedily feast.

She didn't think about the fact that she'd gone so far past subtle flirting she was lost somewhere that she'd never visited and possibly would never wanted to leave. She didn't think about the fact that there would surely be consequences once Jared remembered what he was doing and who he was doing it with. Or, that there was someone sitting at the table beside them, or about the rest of the diners. She didn't think at all. Not until the moan forming at the back of her throat escaped and she was suddenly, unceremoniously, set free and left teetering on her heels.

Breathing hard, not knowing what to do about the completely new and assessing look in Jared's eyes, she glanced about her in desperation.

In the absence of any other idea she reached across the table, picked up his chopsticks, dunked some food in sweet chilli dipping sauce and placed the whole lot in her mouth.

As the silence stretched unbearably Amanda frowned at Jared's

Latest Limpet. She'd expected indignant shock at the kiss, not quickly masked confusion and then the same carefully blank expression that Jared was usually so good at. Then, suddenly, Jared did what he was famous for; taking control.

'Amanda Gray,' his British accent clipped out, 'Meet Leonora King—Nora. My sister.'

Amanda couldn't be sure, but she thought she might just have emitted a thoroughly unladylike snort. But with every synapse short-circuited after the kiss, she could be forgiven, right? His words began to truly register, as she picked up on the tension emanating from Jared and the woman sitting across from him. She became uncomfortably aware of her stupid heart beginning a very definite journey north to her mouth. Swallowing hard, she managed, 'You're serious?' At the woman's perfectly pleasant smile she sat down at the table with a jolt and turned an accusatory stare to the man sat beside her. 'You let me think this woman was one of your...' She closed her eyes to aid breathing, thinking; functioning. Well, this was bad on so many levels; to have actually kissed Jared in the first place...

To discover it was in front of his sister!

She couldn't help it, she looked at Nora and then back to Jared and ended up squeaking pathetically, 'You have family?'

She waited for him to confirm, deny; explain. And when only the snap of his shutters responded, disappointment, an emotion she never thought to associate with him, washed over her.

Her mind raced as she realised that in the few years she'd known him, he'd managed to expertly steer any conversation of family back in the UK firmly in another direction. And because it was Jared, who was always so in control, a person didn't think to keep pushing. And hadn't that, she now realised, suited him right down to the ground?

Turning to Nora, she said, 'Great to meet you. So what's the big family secret that's kept this one here from mentioning any of you?'

Jared rose in one swift, fluid motion, 'Right, time for a little chat.

Outside. Excuse us would you sister, dear.' Manacling Amanda's wrist, he headed for the door.

As soon as they were outside Amanda tugged on the hand and was immediately set free.

'Look,' he ground out, 'I don't quite understand what you thought you were doing back there but you can't just—'

Whirling around to face him, she had no idea why *he* was so angry. 'Okay did you, or did you not, send me one of your emergency texts?'

'I did.' He folded his arms and adopted his usual intractable stance and she hung onto the fact that she wasn't obliged to quake in her boots—not when she was more intrigued by what had him so riled.

'And do they not usually mean 'Help, I can't get rid of my girlfriend'?'

'They do. Usually. But then, usually, you at least wait until I introduce you before you start improvising. What the hell were you thinking?'

'What was I thinking?' she repeated, bemused. 'Given that you sent your usual text and not something more helpful like, oh, maybe, "my sister is in town and I would love it if you could join us for lunch."' She took a step closer, all the better to read him. But he was giving nothing away and she felt her own anger start to spiral. 'How was I supposed to know your text was more of a moral-support code? How was I supposed to know you even had a sister? Next you'll be telling me you have parents, other siblings—the whole shebang.' She watched as the muscle in his jaw clicked rigid.

'It's complicated.'

Her mouth dropped open. Why did she feel so insulted? And jealous! Just because they shared all those long talks over Mikey's hospital bed, did she really think that she was finally getting to know him? 'Well, I guess I wouldn't know about complicated families, would I?'

'That's not the point.'

'It's not? We're not talking about the fact that you need to send out for reinforcements to talk to a sister no one even knows you have? What are we talking about then? The kiss?'

'We're talking,' Jared argued, 'About the fact that you're going to have to stop breezing through life as if nothing matters, without a plan and with total disregard for how your go-with-the-flow attitude might affect others.'

Amanda could only stare as a strange numbing quality began to take hold. Okay, so her visit hadn't heralded the outcome he'd hoped for. He was addled; upset—she got that. But to deliberately hurt her!

'Why are you dressed like that, anyway?' he blurted out in obvious frustration.

'I was at an interview, you jerk.'

'An interview?' A look of sudden understanding passed over his face, 'So Mikey finally told you? I guess that's something at least. Look, I know he and Janey have said they want to get married as soon as possible but you don't need to move out straight away. You have time to get a job you really want.'

'Wait, back up,' Amanda didn't understand. Mikey and Janey were engaged? Since when? And then, as she stood opposite him, feeling like the only one not in on the joke, what Jared was saying slowly started to sink in, 'This is why you offered me the job!' The flush of humiliation was swift and all-encompassing. 'I couldn't possibly get a decent enough job to move into a place of my own! You think I need looking after? Like some child? When it's been me who's taken care of Mikey for years?' Amanda had never felt more stupid in all her twenty-four years. That the two of them had so obviously been discussing what to do about her, when, actually she'd been developing her own plans, thank you very much.

Jared closed the distance between them. Looking deep into her eyes, he blew what little cool she had left about her straight out of the water. 'Amanda, Mikey hasn't needed looking after for a long time. You know that. You know that's not why you stay. You stay because you're too afrai—'

'Don't!' Her voice thick with emotion, her self-preservation had her laying trembling fingertips against his lips. Because if he came right out and said it, if he actually called her a coward, she'd lose it. 'Seriously, you do not get to call on me for help and then call me out for the manner in which I provide it and follow it up by questioning my motives for sticking by my only family.'

As he opened his mouth to speak she pressed harder against his incredible soft lips. His hand came up to grasp hold of her wrist. His eyes bored into hers and she felt his thumb brush against the sensitive pulse point of her wrist. Electricity zinged through her even as she wondered how it could be that she was standing outside on a bitter cold day arguing with her friend. Her friend. who stood in front of her, so in control, whilst everything about her interaction with him since she'd walked into the restaurant had so clearly and irrevocably got away from her.

Her pulse spiked at the continued stroke of his thumb and as his eyes lowered to concentrate on her lips it went haywire. 'Jared?'

The broken whisper of his name on her lips brought him out of his trance-like state and immediately he dropped her hand and stepped backwards. 'You are hereby released from all "Code Red" duty.'

Before she could form words he turned and walked back inside to where Nora was standing centre-stage of the restaurant's plate-glass window doing a reasonable goldfish impression.

Staring at his retreating back, Amanda swore she could hear those damn shutters of his face slamming shut, and a thousand locks being deployed for good measure.

Confusion coursed through her, giving rise to a whole host of elemental emotions.

Jared had sounded as though he'd made some sort of resolution for removing her from more than "Code Red" duty. Interestingly, with the feel of his lips on hers still lingering, she was tempted to tell him that resolutions were made for breaking.

But what with them being friends, though, and what with her promising herself that this year was all about concentrating on her plan, she definitely shouldn't do that.

Should she?

Chapter Two

'What in hell do you think you were doing kissing Jared?'

At the sound of her brother's voice, Amanda pushed the front door shut and slowly turned to face him. It had been hours since the whole knock-her-on-her-ass kiss, followed by the, who-are-you-to-call-me-on-my-deepest-fear 'thing' and truth be told, she was still in a state of shock.

And now it appeared Jared had followed The Best Friend Code to the letter and confessed to Mikey.

Unreasonably annoyed all over again, she really would have preferred Jared to have ignored his sense of honour in favour of returning any one of *her* phone calls.

Sinking back against the solid wood of the door, she needed the warmth of the room to permeate and help soothe her rattled nerves. 'Mikey, I'm cold and I'm tired, do we really have to get into this now?' She couldn't quite look at him and in the interests of hiding the guilt and confusion she knew had to be shining out of her like a beacon, her eyes strayed to the winter coat slung casually over the banister. 'Hey, how did my coat get there?'

'How do you think? Jared dropped it off when he came to tell me my sister had taken leave of her senses.'

'That wasn't *quite* how I put it,' Jared declared as he walked out of the kitchen and came to stand in the hallway.

Heat radiated from Amanda's cheeks. Tempted to fight fire with fire she wanted to demand he tell her exactly how he *had* put it. But under the spell of his quiet regard, she had second, third and fourth thoughts. Crazily, she wondered if she was limber enough to vault the banister, slip on her coat and high-tail it out of the house before Mikey had a chance to whizz his wheelchair around and stop her.

Her need to escape must have shown in her face, because her brother directed a 'Don't even think about it,' at her before looking from her to Jared and back again. Swearing softly under his breath, he said, 'You two obviously have some talking to do,' and wheeled himself off down the hallway.

Talk? Interesting concept. Since Jared had walked away from her she'd walked, stomped and marched for miles; all the while wavering between needing to apologise for her part in whatever it was that had gone on between them earlier and, wanting to instigate round two of whatever it was that had gone on between them earlier. In the end, knowing it had all started with the kiss, the kiss she'd initiated, she'd sucked it up and left countless messages of apology. Now, facing him, that incredible kiss was front and centre and all her stupid tongue seemed capable of doing was cleaving to the roof of her mouth.

'I bought pastries from Luigi's,' Jared offered up patiently. 'Coffee would seem appropriate.'

Slowly, she pushed away from the door to pass him and head into the kitchen. Jared reached for her at the last moment and swung her gently to face him. 'I got your messages. Don't worry about it. Seriously,' he pressed when she turned remorseful eyes on him. 'I was in a weird place and I was way too hard on you. It didn't even register until later that you hadn't known about Mikey and Janey getting engaged.'

For some reason his trying to let her off the hook for kissing him brought an ache to her chest. She settled on the other hurt. 'I can't believe he hasn't told me,' she whispered.

'It's not what you're thinking.' He ran a reassuring hand gently down her arm. She looked down at his hand at her wrist, felt a strong rush of need and hated herself for feeling it. She saw Jared frown uncomfortably at his action, before removing his hand and gesturing for her to precede him into the kitchen. 'Mikey knows you'll be happy for him, he just thought you'd been acting a little differently lately—thought maybe he should wait a while.'

The interviews.

She had been acting differently. Or at least trying to. Ever since she'd opened her eyes and really looked at her brother's new life.

For Mikey, she'd thought ahead.

She'd taken a good hard look at her own life and fought the apprehension that came with putting plans into place.

She'd been hoping the fact that it was New Year, when everyone made plans and lists and promises, would make it look as though changing things wasn't a big deal for her but she obviously hadn't succeeded. She was going to have to try harder.

She set her bag down on a kitchen counter top and reached over to retrieve a couple of small plates from the old oak dresser. Setting mugs out while coffee brewed, she asked, 'What have you done with your sister?'

'She's at a hotel. She was tired after her flight.'

Amanda wanted to know why Nora wasn't sharing his four-bedroom penthouse apartment, but instead of prying she turned and walked over to the island unit where he'd pulled out a bar stool to sit down on. She passed him a plate, a mug of coffee and shoved the pastry box towards him before pulling out her own seat at the opposite end of the unit.

'She seems nice,' she ventured.

Jared shrugged and said nothing for a moment. 'So, what was your interview for?'

Amanda nibbled away at her pastry and pretended to have great interest in stirring her coffee. In the same way it appeared Jared was disinclined to talk about his sister, she felt disinclined to talk

17

about her interview.

Glancing up she caught him focusing on her lips. Heat flooded her, warming her better than any hot drink could have done and in a bid to steer their focus elsewhere, she said, 'Tell me about Nora and I'll tell you about my interview.'

Jared smiled briefly and lowered his mug to the granite work surface. 'There's nothing much to tell. Apart from the obvious shock of seeing her,' he paused, as if debating how much he should say. 'We've not been in touch for some years.'

Baffled, Amanda wondered how and why a person went about losing contact with their family. But one look at his face and, okay, she knew she was going to have to leave it alone, lest she spook him back into silence.

'Your interview?' he prompted.

She reached out to trace a sparkle in the granite. 'There's nothing much to tell,' she mimicked and then sighed, 'It was for a PA at an art gallery, but I think I was over-reaching somewhat.'

'You don't think you might be doing yourself a bit of a disservice?'

'Jared, I work three days a week as a barista,' she looked at him as if that explained everything and when he merely politely stared back at her she added, 'I never re-started my degree after Mikey's rehabilitation,' she looked down at her hands. 'I've coasted. You practically said so yourself earlier.'

'I should never have said anything. I was...out of sorts. I'm slightly concerned you feel unworthy of something I have every faith you can get, though. Why do you think I offered you a job in the first place?'

Her throat clogged with instant emotion and it seemed a good time to go back to tracing the fascinating patterns in the work surface. 'You offered me a job because of Mikey.'

'I offered you a job because I've seen what you've achieved around this place. I've seen you juggle working part time with a difficult renovation and what has seemed like endless filling out of insurance forms and grants for Mikey's rehabilitation. I offered you a job because you seemed ready,' he paused. 'But maybe I was wrong.'

'You? Wrong? Not possible!' She looked into knowing eyes and felt her shoulders slump. 'I need to show Mikey I can do this.'

'The only person you need to prove anything to—is yourself.'

'Sure. That's what I meant.' She took a deep breath and fixed him with her best can-do expression. 'It's why you can relax about having to offer me employment. The interview this morning was just a blip on an otherwise fail-safe plan.'

'Wait, you have a plan? *You* do?'

'What? It's not beyond the realms of possibility.'

'It kind of is, actually. You have many skills, but putting together a Life Plan?' Jared gave a mock shudder and Amanda regretted seating herself so far away because it meant landing a swift left hook was currently outside her physical scope. But, darn it, he was right. Again. She knew she gave every impression of abhorring making plans. Life had this way of sneaking up and upsetting any she made, so it made total sense to her to avoid making them.

Avoid disappointment. Avoid upset.

Going with the flow was a perfectly acceptable lifestyle choice and, perversely, made her feel in control. Of course, if she could just get Life to stop throwing her curveballs in the first place she'd be more willing to make nice with The Planning Gremlins.

'Maybe I should take a look at this plan for you, check it's not really more of a list, because,' Jared broke off and glanced towards her bag, suddenly emitting noise. 'You want to answer your phone?'

Amanda shook her head. So much for hoping he'd politely ignore the fact that her phone was ringing with all the subtlety of the clanging chimes of doom.

'It could be about your interview.'

It was definitely going to be about the interview. Her luck said it was the agency ringing her with a 'no'. A word she suddenly didn't want to hear. Not after owning up to her plan. Not if it would make her look as if she'd fallen at the first hurdle. Not if it made her wish she'd accepted Jared's job offer in the first place.

A job offer that was now completely off the table.

On account of the whole sizzling kissing thing.

With leaden feet she crossed to her bag and rummaged for her phone. Answering it she turned her back on Jared and listened to the agency telling her the gallery owner had decided to go with someone with more experience.

As she felt her head drop she determinedly set her shoulders. This was not the end of the world. This was a new year, a new her. So she'd line up some more interviews. Pursue her plan.

Feel the fear and do it anyway.

She returned her phone to her bag and turned around.

'It was a "no"?' Jared asked.

She nodded.

'Their loss,' he commiserated, giving her all of ten seconds to sit back down at the table before getting up and walking around to her side of the unit and saying in a low voice, 'You could always revisit my proposition.'

Her body instantly responded to the chocolate pitch of his voice. 'Pr-proposition?' she questioned lamely.

'Mmmn.' He smiled down at her, plucked the mugs from the table and dunked them both in the kitchen sink along with the pastry dishes. He turned on the taps and Amanda wished mightily for a cold shower.

'Accept my job offer and come to London with me.'

'London?' Amanda gaped. 'London?' Glad his back was to her, she tried to get a hold of her runaway thoughts, realising that for an instant she had committed the cardinal sin of associating Jared with an altogether different kind of proposition. Bad idea, she scolded herself. Very. Bad. Idea.

'I need to go back to London and I need a Personal Assistant to accompany me.'

'Oh. Okay. Let me just pack a bag,' she said crossing her eyes comically behind him, 'wait, what shall we tell Janey—that she's taken one too many coffee breaks and you're through with her?' She slid off the stool to come and stand next to him.

'I need Janey here keeping an eye on things. And she and Mikey could do with the time together.'

Amanda picked up a mug and a dishtowel. 'So what's in London?' she asked.

For a moment, when Jared simply stared at his hands submerged in the soapy water, she thought he wasn't going to respond.

When he did, his words were dragged from deep within. 'A sick father and a failing family business.'

Amanda put the mug down and stretched her hand out in an automatic offer of comfort. 'This is what your sister came to tell you?' She felt the corded sinew of his forearm harden beneath her fingers.

'It's-'

'Complicated?' she helped, sure his hands had formed fists beneath the water's surface.

He turned to look at her. He was absolutely still and yet she could sense something coursing through him—that edge of danger; a flash of fire in otherwise cool, clear green eyes.

'Complicated is an understatement.' He did that quiet thinking thing and from his expression she knew he was weighing up the consequences of revealing something to her. 'I'm sure my sister would be only too happy to provide me with one of her assistants but I'd rather take someone I know with me; someone without ulterior motive.'

Unbidden she saw herself tasting his lips, and flustered, felt the ridiculous need for him to clarify what he was asking of her. 'And I'd be in London as your Personal Assistant?'

'Amanda, you could do the job standing on your head.'

She stared up at him, gripping the kitchen roll top as casually as she could manage because suddenly his utter belief in her had her wanting to take the risk and go with him. He was that sure of her? It had her wanting to repay his compliment by offering whatever support he needed.

She swallowed. 'How exactly would you go about telling your sister that in one day I've gone from "sleeping" with you to working for you?'

'It's none of her business.'

Right. That shut down that then. She was going to have to actually come out and say it wasn't she? 'Speaking of,' she moved a hand between them, 'you know, the—' she couldn't say it.

'—Kiss?' His eyes moved to her lips and she had to fight an insane urge to moisten them with the tip of the tongue. 'Forget about it.' He withdrew his hands from the water and reached for the dishtowel she was still holding. 'Are you going to let fear rule your life, then?'

'What do you mean?' she spluttered, pinned under his searching gaze.

'I know you're capable of more than you have let your life become. You say you're ready to change your life. Prove it.'

That was exactly what she was trying to do. She just needed one person to take a chance on her, to believe she could do a job without having recent experience to back it up. It slowly dawned on her that there was someone standing right in front of her completely willing to take that risk. And, actually, how awesome would it be to prove to him she was worth taking a chance on? Purely in a work capacity, of course.

'Mikey's going to think your moving out is a lot less a knee-jerk reaction to change if you do it sensibly and with thought,' Jared added. 'Like dipping your toe in the water with a temporary assignment that will give you money towards a place of your own, a reference you can take to your next position. What's to think about anyway?' he cajoled, 'Use that go-with-the-flow mentality of yours. Snap up the opportunity and let it open some doors for you. I'll even help you come up with a proper plan for after.'

Oh he was good; this man practically had a degree in planning.

So good that as her mind began processing the permutations, she realised she was genuinely considering his offer. Suddenly all she could see were benefits. Like the fact that Mikey could enjoy some time with Janey without his little sister being in the way. Like the fact Jared wouldn't have to face family he was so obviously estranged from alone. Like the fact she'd get good work experience and a reference and savings to kick-start her search for a job when she came home.

And yet, well, there was still the elephant in the room.

Honestly why she had to keep harping on about it she didn't know, but she licked her lips and tried again. 'About the kiss—'

Jared regarded her unflinchingly. 'What about it? So the Code Red thing got a little out of hand. We'll learn from it. The kiss was fun but misguided. It wasn't us. We're friends. That's all.'

That's all?

Of *course* that was all. Why would Jared want or need it to be anything else? Why did she, come to think of it?

If he could discount it so easily, and be so sure that it wouldn't be an issue, why couldn't she?

***

Jared looked up from his papers, realising he'd read through half a document and couldn't recall the first thing about it. He was way too aware of his new Personal Assistant. She was sitting on the cream leather seat opposite him, chuntering delightfully to herself as she fiddled with the phone he'd casually thrown at her as they'd boarded the private jet bound for London.

'Having trouble operating it?' he asked with a smile on his face.

'No, merely concerned about the trail of sobbing women we seem to have left behind. Every single call on this thing has been from women eager to know if you're available. I think I'm going to have to set up some sort of helpline while you're out of the country.'

His smile widened and an edge of wickedness crept in. 'I may have given you my private phone by mistake.'

'You have more than one?' Her mouth formed a perfect 'O' of surprise that he really oughtn't to find so appealing. 'What am I talking about? Of course you have more than one.' She glanced about the jet's interior, looking a little pale. 'Please tell me you don't have more than one of these babies?'

'As it happens this one belongs to the family. But relax. It's just stuff—'

'Sure,' she agreed with an exaggerated nod, 'Stuff.'

'There's absolutely no reason to be intimidated. It's a mode of transport. That's all.'

'Uh-huh. One beautiful pimped-up mode of transport.'

She ran her fingertip over the leather before reaching out to trace the walnut veneer of the drinks table. Why had he never noticed she had a tendency to drag her fingertip over different surfaces? It was as if nothing was real until she touched it. He found it disconcertingly sexy; seductive.

Idly, he wondered what he'd have to do to get her to drag a fingertip over him in such an exploratory way, then with a start realised he had absolutely, categorically, no business wondering any such thing. Her fingers moved into her sleek caramel-brown ponytail, stroking over the length of it. Suddenly parched, he reached for his scotch.

'I guess I feel a little under-prepared,' she said. 'I mean, it wasn't as if I didn't know you were a successful businessman or that you worked hard and reaped the rewards. I'm just a little embarrassed I never realised *how* successful you were.'

'I'm not where I want to be *just* yet.' The words came automatically. He thought about the deal he was halfway through making. To leave at such a crucial stage irritated the hell out of him, but Nora's second pitch had been perfect and to his astonishment he'd found himself changing his answer from a 'no' to a 'yes'. It had to have been the shock of kissing Amanda.

Kissing Amanda.

Two words; one sentence, that had the power to throw him properly off kilter.

After the hell of Mikey's accident and the guilt from knowing he was responsible, no matter what Mikey said...Amanda had continued to treat him the same way she always had. As if he had a clean sheet. It was addictive and liberating and, when he let himself actually think about it, selfish; down-to-the-bone selfish. And had him doubting she understood the luxury he found her company to be.

Amanda, whose sassiness challenged him, whose over-the-top disdain for his planned approach to life amused him.

But then he'd gone and returned her kiss.

He'd told himself he'd re-offered her the job as a way of compensating for her losing out on an interview that could have bettered her situation. He'd told himself that by persuading her to accept he'd be showing Mikey he could be trusted with her. He'd told himself over and over that the kiss had been a fluke. There was no possible way that someone, so opposite to him in outlook, could produce such a primal response from a place so deep inside of him he'd forgotten it even existed.

She'd made him feel like he'd come home.

What a joke. Home was a place he no longer deserved.

He turned his head to look out of the jet's small window and beyond, through the thin layers of cloud, to the earth below.

He'd been given back the keys to The House of King but The *Home* of King? He'd be mad to think that was in the bricks and mortar of the forty-acre estate just outside of London. No, the true King home was the business premises of King Property Corporation—KPC headquarters in the heart of the City. When Nora had surrendered those clunky-as-hell keys during her deftly argued invitation, he had been more bewildered than he cared to admit.

It seemed the prodigal son was expected to ride to the rescue.

He felt the automatic grimace. Thinking about KPC and his father had him wound tighter than anything else ever could. No wonder thinking about Amanda was such a welcome distraction.

Taking another sip from the crystal tumbler he tried not to let his eyes slide over her legs. Instead, he dragged his gaze back to her button-brown eyes.

'Like I said, this is just stuff.' He paused. 'I suppose I'd better warn you. London may be a little...more, than this.'

She whistled softly under her breath and looked around once more. 'Okay. So essentially what you're telling me is that I was a fool to turn down your, at the time insulting, but I now realise practical, offer of dressing me for this job, given that your family are rich and I'm about to look thoroughly out of place?'

'What you have on is fine.'

More than fine. The simple royal-blue shift and matching heels transformed her into a sleek, confident career woman, who now looked way too grown up, way too sophisticated, way too hot and way too available. Somehow he thought he'd be safer if she was back in the usual gypsy-like clothes she wore. At least there'd be less smooth skin on show.

'But they are—you are...rich?' she tentatively asked.

He inclined his head a fraction.

'Lord. How rich? Like they invented money, rich?'

Jared pursed his lips to stop the smile from growing.

'Oh, you are in such trouble, mister. Right, I need a complete etiquette run-down pronto. Make every word count or I'll probably be thrown out the country before we even set down.'

Jared leaned forward in his seat, 'You don't need any kind of run-down. You'll be absolutely fine. There are no mistakes you can make that could be seen as not done in King company because you are not there for the King family. You're there for me. You don't answer to anyone but me and if *anyone* upsets you or asks you to do something you feel isn't appropriate you tell me and I will sort it out.'

From Amanda's raised eyebrow he realised he may have gone a little over the top. Her large brown eyes bore into him and then slowly she reached out to get her flute of champagne. She took a long, slow sip and remained silent. A good tactic, he realised, as it made him feel as though he should explain himself.

'Look. I just don't want you to feel that all of the stuff that comes with the name is more important than it actually is, or that it's designed as a way of intimidating a person.'

Amanda leant forward in her seat, her ringless hands dangling the champagne flute delicately in front of her.

'Jared, why haven't you seen your family for so long? If I don't understand at least some of it how can I have your back? And that is, primarily, why I'm here, isn't it—to have your back? I'm the extra eyes and ears. If you just wanted someone to make appointments for you, you could have brought over one of your lim—' she stopped and brought the glass hurriedly to her lips.

'One of my what?'

'Limpets,' she said defiantly.

'You call my girlfriends Limpets?' He didn't know whether to be amused or horrified.

'Don't change the subject.'

Jared leant back in his chair.

How did one explain ten years of no contact or the ugly year preceding it? Badly, he guessed.

'I haven't seen my family since the day I was no longer considered King business material and as a consequence no longer considered King family material.'

'The two are synonymous?'

'Where my father's concerned? Absolutely.' He tried to keep the bitterness out of his voice. One look at her stricken expression and he wasn't entirely certain he'd managed it.

Amanda gradually became aware her mouth was hanging open. 'You were kicked out of your own family? I don't get it; you have more integrity than any man I know.' Had that been the wrong thing to say? Something fierce flashed in his eyes but then he blinked and it was gone.

'I was a spoilt, irresponsible, selfish young man who bought shame on the family name.'

'Baloney!'

'There isn't any one part of that statement that isn't true.'

'No way!'

'No?'

She didn't like the way he was so convincing and had a feeling that at any moment the shutters would fall. She took another sip of champagne and thought for a second before speaking.

'Okay, well...so now you're going back a changed man. A successful businessman with a reputation for being forward-thinking, shrewd, and above all, fair. What?' she asked, taking in his half-smile, 'so I did some research, read a few articles. The point is, even if what you say is true, and I don't for one minute think it's the whole truth, you're now older, wiser and more mature. Your father will be proud.'

She wanted desperately to take that glint out of his eyes. The one that told her he thought she was being naive. She didn't want to be thought of as naive by him. She wanted to be thought of as the voice of reason. But there was still so much she didn't understand.

'He won't be proud of the fact that you went into the same line of business?' She watched the quick shrug of his shoulders and couldn't determine whether Jared didn't care if his father was proud, or deliberately didn't care that he might not be. 'Well, isn't it lucky for him that you did—the fact that he needs your help now—'

'Oh, I doubt he even knows of Nora's rescue mission.'

'So, I guess this whole trip is going to be trickier than I realised, but you've probably been working on those plans of yours twenty-four-seven. I trust you.' Her eyes bounced off the stack of documents between them and up to study the strong features of his face. She looked into his eyes and suddenly the atmosphere in the small jet felt charged, as if they'd passed through an electrical storm.

'Are you sure you should?'

She watched him watching her as she brought the champagne hastily to her lips and took a healthy last swallow. 'Don't be ridiculous. Of course I trust you.' Once again his green eyes sparked with something she didn't understand, and quickly turned inscrutable. 'Want to hear *my* plan?' she said, aiming for some light humour.

'*Your* plan?' Jared mocked.

She tipped her head, touché. 'Proposal then. I propose we land, settle in, you have a few deep-and-meaningfuls with the family, a board meeting is convened, you present your plan to save the company and then tomorrow? Well, I hear the shopping is fantastic.'

Jared was silent a moment. He swirled the remaining amber liquid in his glass, considering. In one smooth motion he downed the last mouthful and she distinctly heard the last piece of ice being crunched between his teeth. He grinned.

'Do you know in all my figuring out the angles, that wasn't the way I ended up going.'

'It wasn't?' Why did she have a funny feeling? Her hand pressed gently over the butterflies flitting about inside her stomach.

'Well for a start who said anything about *saving* KPC?'

The tiny air-pocket that the jet hit, causing Amanda to be lifted slightly and then set down abruptly in her seat, was nothing compared with the shock of Jared's statement and the ruthless edge she didn't recognise.

Chapter Three

'You've gone mad.' Amanda accused, struggling to keep up with him. She barely registered the plush private airport lounge as they proceeded towards the exit at what seemed like a hundred miles an hour. 'You're out of your mind.'

'Why? For putting a failing business out of its misery?'

'But, it's not just *any* business; it's the family business. And it would be for all the wrong reasons.'

If she had thought for one minute he'd asked her to travel thousands of miles to help him push the final nail into an eighty-year-old family business, just because he hadn't been allowed to be a part of it, she would never have come. There were few things she stood firm on. Family was family. 'Jared, you are *not* about wrong reasons. *You* are about right reasons. Hey,' she finally managed to get a half step in front of him, and as her hand shot out to stop him in his tracks it landed full square on his chest, right over his heart. She kept it there as she spoke. 'As I was saying, you are all about integrity. Fact: the friendship you share with Mikey is based on just that—friendship and *not* because you feel responsible for his accident.' She felt his heart thump solidly against his chest. Finally, she had his attention. 'I see you struggling with that some-times and yet you never let it get in the way. You don't think I had to wrestle with, and let go of, the fact you paid Mikey's medical bills and for the house to be specially adapted?' She pushed back against his hard chest when he made to step forward. 'If you tell me you did that solely out of guilt, I think I'll hate you!' He blinked and she pressed her advantage. The shutters came down but his heart was still thumping. 'If you do this, just because you can, what does that say about you?'

'You have absolutely no idea what you are talking about.'

'So then, explain it to me. Family is family, Jared.'

'Family is not always family. Family is sometimes—' but then Jared broke off to stare ahead of them. 'Sephy?' he called out softly.

Frowning, Amanda followed his gaze in time to see a beautiful woman with flowing jet-black hair jog towards him. She was carrying an equally beautiful toddler.

'Jared—' the woman broke off; seemingly at a loss for words but then someone wriggled in her arms and a smile lit up her face. 'This is Daisy; my daughter,' she said proudly, offering a giggling Daisy up for inspection.

Amanda looked at the stunned expression on Jared's face and when it became apparent he was incapable of speech, she stepped in.

'I'm Amanda, Jared's PA.' She reached out to stroke a fingertip over Daisy's chubby forearm. 'Hello, Daisy.'

Jared's eyes lingered on Amanda's outstretched finger before he slowly seemed to collect himself.

'Amanda, this is my other sister Seraphina—Sephy, and, er, her daughter.' He shot questioning eyes to his sister and Amanda realised that he hadn't even known he was an uncle.

Maybe he was right. Maybe family wasn't always family as she understood it. She only had Mikey since their parents had died and they were such a unit, she couldn't envisage being strangers, the way Jared and his sisters had so obviously become. She wanted badly to place her hand in his and offer a squeeze of comfort, but was fairly certain that PA's didn't do that.

'Okay, I'm confused,' Sephy said. 'Nora gave me the impression you were Jared's—'

'No,' Amanda hastily cut in. 'Not at all. There was a gargantuan mix-up on my part when I met your sister. We're strictly professional. Er, that is, we have a strictly professional relationship.' She shot a look towards Jared that said, 'Pull yourself together and help me dig myself out of this hole, will you?' and it seemed to work, because from out of nowhere Jared grinned, Daisy gurgled and Sephy chuckled.

'No problem.' Sephy assured. 'I have a car waiting to take us back to the house.'

'Amanda and I are not staying at the house.'

Sephy instantly plopped Daisy down beside her and reached for her phone. She punched in a number and managed to grab Daisy before the toddler could shoot off.

'Nora? You were right. Er,' she looked up at Jared with a question on her face and he sighed and took the phone from her.

Amanda watched him take control with natural ease. Could she find a way to get him to at least look at the business before he waltzed in and pronounced it beyond saving? Was it really her place? He was the expert here, not her. Most definitely not her, she thought, feeling the nerves start to gather.

She glanced at Sephy and Daisy. They were watching Jared; rapt fascination on their faces and she had to smile. He tended to have that effect on people. She tuned back in and heard him say, 'Well you'll have to find a new plan then...I'm glad you understand. I'll tell her.' He snapped the phone shut, 'She said to tell you to go ahead with Plan B,' looking at Amanda he said, 'We'll be staying at Nora's apartment in the City. She's staying elsewhere.'

Her nervous feelings doubled as she acknowledged an underlying zing of excitement. Wasn't the property in the UK supposed to be all small and poky? Wouldn't they end up all on top of one another? Her eyes grew wide at the Technicolor graphic her imagination supplied. Realising Jared was looking at her oddly she rallied herself, smiling benignly when his eyebrow raised in query.

She had to get a proper grip of herself. What did she care if plans changed and she wasn't staying in the sprawling formal country estate with space to spare? She was Amanda go-with-the-flow Gray. No sweat. No problem.

Later, travelling in the lift up to Nora's penthouse apartment, Amanda tried to stave off the mounting apprehension as to what Jared would say to her when they were alone. Surely she'd over-stepped the mark when she'd virtually accused him of deliberately hanging the family business out to dry?

Before she could dwell too much on his reaction, the lift doors opened onto acres of creamy deep-piled carpet. Light pooled in through floor-to-ceiling windows that framed a view of the city.

'Oh. Wow.' Amanda walked over to stare at the London skyline, desperate to grab her camera and guide book out of her bag and run off and explore.

She turned to find Jared watching her with a soft smile on his face. Her heart missed a beat. He didn't look as though he was holding a grudge. She crossed her eyes comically to show she realised she was being a bit gauche and picked up some of her bags to head off, she hoped, in the direction of the bedrooms.

Choosing the smaller room with its silk, champagne-coloured wallpaper and beautifully polished Venetian furniture, she set about unpacking, content to leave brother, sister and niece to some private time. After storing her toiletries in the sumptuous bathroom she crossed back to the plate-glass window in front of the bed. At night she'd be able to see thousands of artificial lights wobbling back at her from their reflection in the Thames below. Running her hand over the pane, she realised that the intricate skyline was cleverly etched onto the glass. Idly tracing it with her finger, she wondered if the window was redone as the skyline changed. Maybe they didn't have to. Maybe nothing changed here. She shook her head at her naivety; as if London was any different to anywhere else. Everything changed sooner or later. That was why it did no good to plan. Zoning back in to the sound of stilted

33

conversation in the living room area, she went to join them.

'—wait till you see Dad with Daisy,' Sephy was saying. 'She has him wrapped around her little finger and he loves it, doesn't he, Daisy?' Daisy giggled back up at her mother but Amanda was more intrigued by the look of pure disbelief on Jared's face.

'You'll see. You're both invited for dinner, by the way.'

'I'm afraid tonight's out of the question.'

Amanda busied herself searching her capacious handbag for a notebook, but not before she saw a look of disappointment pass over Sephy's face.

'Of course. No rush. You probably have jet lag or something. Um, you may not remember, but Dad always holds a winter party and this year it's on the 26th. You're both welcome.'

'Has he even been told I'm here or why I'm here?'

'Of course. Nora would never have flown over to see you unless father had sanctioned it.'

'Of course,' Jared mimicked.

Amanda winced into her handbag and heard Sephy rush on.

'He knows this is to be conducted on your terms—'

Jared's laugh was tinged with bitterness. 'Tell me, where is the real Jeremy King and what have you done with him?'

In the awkward silence, Amanda's anxious handbag-search became more pronounced.

'The real Jeremy King,' Sephy said through pinched lips, 'is right where he's always been, Jared.' She started stuffing Daisy's bits and bobs into her bag. 'He's not the one who left.' She grabbed up Daisy in her other arm and walked towards the lift.

'*Well stop her, then, idiot.*' For a moment, as Amanda watched Jared's head whip around to his sister's departing back, she thought she'd uttered the words aloud.

But then the lift doors swished shut, leaving Amanda and Jared alone.

Emotion pulled at Jared's features, making the beautiful sculpted bones of his face stand even more proud. Amanda wanted to soothe him, hating she the fact that she didn't know what he needed. She cleared her throat, 'Well. I'm no reunion connoisseur, but under the circumstances I think that went quite well, don't you?'

Jared was busy computing Sephy's parting words. He didn't understand. Could it be that neither of his sisters had been told of what had happened back then? How was that possible?

He shook his head slightly in automatic denial. It was simply inconceivable that his father had been trying to protect him. No, it made more sense that his father was simply protecting his daughters. Better his sisters think ill of their brother and the choices they thought he'd willingly made.

All of a sudden, he felt absolutely shattered.

'Feel like taking a walk?' he asked, raising dead eyes to Amanda.

'Sure, just let me grab my guide book and I'll leave you alone for a couple of hours.'

'No. I meant with me.'

Her smile lit up the room and in the moment he refused to feel guilty that he'd manipulated her into accompanying him on this trip. By way of recompense, he'd make sure she went home with a reference that would get her any job she wanted.

They walked the City's streets and now and then he'd point out a building and give a potted history lesson. She absorbed every word and with each infectious smile he felt his inner turmoil melting away. When was the last time he'd taken time out to admire the buildings he had systematically acquired? When had he forgotten it was the buildings themselves which had first inspired him and not just the simplicity of adding them to his portfolio? Probably around the time he'd realised he was *good* at acquiring things, that he'd inherited some of the King genes after all, and that it would be satisfaction itself if he were able to acquire more in a larger playing field than his father. Then, never again could he be accused of being...

A large raindrop splashed on the bridge of his nose, breaking into his reverie. He looked around for Amanda and found her crouching gracefully under a tree, camera pointing upwards.

'Won't the lens get wet?'

She shrugged her shoulders and motioned for him to adopt a similar stance as she passed the camera to him. 'Look straight up, between those two branches. See the angel from the statue opposite reflected perfectly in the glass of the office block?'

He took the photograph and passed the camera back to her. Not many people would look through something to see what was behind it. 'You've never thought of going professional?'

The shadows passed over her features as she looked at the photo he'd taken, altered some of her settings and took up her position again to take the shot. 'I'd just completed my first year of study when Mikey had his accident.'

'I thought you were studying business?'

'I was. I guess photography was just for fun. You know—something extra.'

She held the camera up to her face again, and then, when he suspected she'd composed herself, lowered it and moved off.

He followed at a slower pace, sighing internally when he realised which building she'd reached.

'So this is where we come tomorrow?'

'Yes.'

Together their eyes swept over the intimidating steel sculpture that spelt out KPC in the foreground of the towering office block. Amanda stepped closer to peer into the lobby at the enormous potted trees and marble reception area, where a security guard sat staring at a bank of screens.

Hunching into his coat, Jared turned and began walking.

He could tell the exact moment she caught up with him; her presence thawing the icicles forming in his veins. He took one step away, trying to protect the ice that was creeping and crawling up his spine. He deserved all the punishing feelings that this particular building evoked. Turning abruptly, he stared at the office tower immediately opposite and felt the same sickening jolt.

He hadn't realised he'd wandered into this particular plaza.

'Wow,' she whispered, 'great combination of office and courtyard.'

He forced himself to stand and stare at the buildings before them.

'It probably still belongs to the King portfolio. It didn't use to look like this,' he turned in a slow circle, searching all the clean lines, the sharp edges; the mix of old and new. 'It's as if none of it ever happened.'

'What never happened?'

Shaking his head, a few water droplets fell, along with the other raindrops. He half-reached out to brush away a raindrop from the corner of Amanda's eye, but she got there first and he was glad he hadn't touched her—in this place that reminded him of his biggest mistake. He saw the confusion in her eyes and attempted a smile, 'Nothing, come on, let's go before we drown.'

***

Amanda stood in the shadows clutching her champagne. The King's home had an actual ballroom in it. For actual balls.

'So this is where you got to. I'm rather concerned by your total disregard for the plan this evening.'

Amanda smiled into her champagne flute and took a healthy sip before turning around to acknowledge Jared's teasing.

'Plan?' She smiled up at him, 'What plan would that be?' She leaned her shoulder against one of the stone pillars supporting the balconied level above them. It was the quietest, darkest part of the beautiful room.

'The one where you were supposed to stick by my side at all times.'

'Ah. That plan.' She risked a little look at him from under her lashes. 'You're not really that surprised, are you?' She'd only been absent a couple of minutes. She had been desperate for a little air; a private moment to mop up the drooling that came with seeing him in his custom-made tuxedo.

'Not really. You've been the very picture of a perfect plan-follower all week. I've been monumentally impressed.' He didn't sound impressed. He sounded peeved. As if he'd found her ability to cope distracting.

All week she'd been working her butt off, hoping he wouldn't regret giving her a chance. And somewhere during hours she hadn't even known existed for work, she'd found herself loving it; beginning to thrive on the structured, systematic audit of the business. Her gut instinct told her the more Jared drilled down into the detail, the more involved with the family business he would become and the better the chances of KPC getting the reprieve they so desperately needed.

She didn't like that her efforts might not have been enough to impress him. 'It's been torture! You know how I love to go with the flow, but I made the effort. Figured you were worth it,' she said outrageously.

'Oh, I'm worth it alright. And your effort will be rewarded.'

Despite the delicious and totally inappropriate shiver that his words prompted, her heart kicked in empathetically. It was impossible not to feel the waves of tension rolling off him. If he wanted her close tonight, well at its most basic level, that's what he was paying her for. She refused to dwell on what that might mean at its most complicated level.

'Shall we, then?' She made to move out of the shadow, but he took a tiny step closer.

'Have I told you how incredible you look?' he asked; his voice deepening as his eyes swept the length of her.

'I expect so,' she answered, aiming for unaffected either way. She closed her eyes briefly, hoping the simple act would somehow allow her to breathe more deeply and relax more fully, because, damn it, she wanted him to think she looked incredible tonight.

The long evening gown of black satin with the band of green, grey, black and silver glass beads just under her breasts, the feel of the silky drape of material against her skin, the backless back with its halter neck tie, the teased curls piled in a loose knot atop her head and the smoky makeup. She'd never looked better. And after the way he'd been sidestepping her all week, something fierce inside her demanded that he acknowledge it.

But now that he had... She should have stopped wanting and started planning. Planning the correct response to the fact that Jared was only flirting as a distraction from the real reason they were here tonight.

Meeting his father.

'Damn, I hate to be predictable,' he said with a sexy side-grin.

'Liar,' she laughed nervously.

'You're so sure I can't step beyond the constraints of predict-ability?' He ran a hand almost idly down her arm, clasped her hand and slowly brought her forefinger to his mouth and ran it feather-soft along the seam of his lips. His tongue brushed against the tip of her finger and as she breathed in sharply his green eyes went dark and smoky. He guided her hand down the lapel of his suit jacket to circle one of the buttons. 'I can do spontaneous.'

'Jared, stop it.' She tried to wrestle her hand free but he wasn't letting go. His thumb brushed over the pulse point at her wrist and everything inside her yielded.

'Stop what?' He searched her eyes, daring her to say what was on her mind.

'You know what. This. I know why you're doing it. I mean, I understand. I'm a distraction. You're nervous. Worried. Feeling out of your comfort zone—'

'Sweet.' His smile was without humour, implying he found her answer anything but.

'It's counter-productive. It's only winding you tighter, and if you must know, it's making *me* nervous as hell.'

He looked down at her, this time a devilish smile playing at the corner of his lips. 'Well, we can't have that. Kiss me for luck?'

Amanda was quite certain she'd have retorted with suitable

pith if it hadn't been for the fact that as soon as she opened her mouth to speak, he swooped down to slide his lips hotly over hers. His quiet, guttural moan and the hot sweep of his tongue had her mouth opening wider and her heart thumping erratically against her ribs before soaring out of her to dip and glide merrily through the stratosphere.

Lord. The man had moves. Real, heart-stopping, stomach-dropping, toe-curling, finger-clenching, body-needing-support moves.

With hands arrogantly shoved in his pockets, the only part of his body touching her was his mouth. His lips rubbed against hers with velvet promise. Tasting, parting, clinging. Claiming.

'Jared.'

'Ssh. I'm being spontaneous.' His hands came out of his pockets to drive into her hair and bring her more fully against him. 'God, you kiss like an angel.'

'Son?'

Jared's head snapped up and the breath rushed out of his lungs. He blinked, swore and took a step backwards and Amanda moaned at the loss of contact. She didn't understand.

And then she did. Oh Lord, did she! This kissing Jared in front of members of his family simply had to stop. She mentally slapped her forehead. Wasn't she supposed to, now she could recall the thousand lectures she'd sternly given her knowing reflection earlier that evening, stick to her vow of acting professionally? She was pretty sure that nixed kissing Jared completely.

She took a surreptitious step from behind Jared's protective stance to stand at his side. Jeremy King looked not at all like she'd imagined, and she realised she'd pictured an older version of Jared.

The man before them was of average height, with sandy brown hair peppered with grey. Despite the physical differences, there was no mistaking that same magnetic presence, borne of generations of wealth and entitlement coupled with the experience of running large organisations. Like Jared, it didn't seem to Amanda as if Jeremy often had to explain himself.

The room quietened imperceptibly as if sensing two powerful forces were about to face-off. She started to panic. As deep-down angry with Jared as she was, that he could so successfully employ her as a distraction and have her respond so easily, she still didn't want for him to become the entertainment portion of the evening.

She should have thought about the proceedings tonight, at least taken responsibility for ensuring that the first time his father laid eyes on his son it wasn't to find him in a compromising position.

Jared shoved his hands back into his pockets. Amanda felt the tension notch up as Jeremy noticed his son's action and after a heartbeat, casually mirrored it.

'You've spoken with your mother?'

'This morning on the phone.'

He had? Amanda had been fielding calls for him all day. He must have initiated contact. That was good, wasn't it?

'I thought you would arrive early in order to talk before guests arrived.'

'I decided to forgo the hastily dusted-off welcome mat in favour of the red-carpet treatment that your other guests would get.'

'You're not a guest, Jared, you're family.'

Amanda both heard and felt Jared draw breath and with sirens clanging in her head hastily stepped between the two.

'I'm afraid our late arrival was completely my fault.' She held her hand out in introduction, refusing to drop it during the wait Jeremy King subjected her to before reaching for her hand and shaking it firmly. 'I'm Amanda Gray.' Her gaze never wavered as she said, 'Your house is exquisite. I'm thinking a house as exquisite as this is bound to have some sort of private study, handy for your average awkward family reunion?'

Jeremy King's laugh was genuine, if a long time coming. 'An innovative suggestion. Jared? Shall we?' And with utter confidence he turned and headed off through the crowd.

Taking her cue Amanda stepped in the opposite direction. 'Good luck,' she whispered and because she couldn't help herself, leant in to brush her lips across his cheek. With a quick waggle of her fingers she turned to walk away.

'Wait.' His hand shot out to grasp hers. 'Long gone are the days when my father gets to click his fingers and expect I'll follow. Let him wait a while.'

'Or, you could go another way and just get this first meeting over with as quickly as possible. Come on, you're in London. In his house. At his party. The only way this was ever going to go was awkwardly. This way at least it's in private. You don't need an audience this first time. It's better just you and him. Hear him out. Say your piece. Just, you know, try not to kill each other. It'd put a real downer on the party atmosphere!' And pulling her fingers free as gently as she could, she walked off into the crowd.

Forty minutes later Jared left his father's private study feeling hollow and restless; his only coherent thought: finding Amanda. He needed... no; he couldn't allow himself to need anything from Amanda. What he *wanted* from her; that was more basic. Easier to understand. And completely out of the question. He shouldn't have kissed her earlier. Because aside from the fact she was his best friend's sister, she was also a friend in her own right. And being friends trumped being two consenting adults. Didn't it? He stopped short. Of course it did.

He needed to regain some semblance of control. Then maybe he'd be able to deal with the fact that his father was gravely ill. Deal with the fact that the forgiveness he'd expected on either side hadn't as yet transpired. Deal with keeping Amanda in the box marked 'friend'.

Spotting her back of bare, flawless, creamy skin he retrieved a glass of champagne from a passing waiter and walked towards her.

As if especially attuned to him she turned, the long dangle of her earring trickling tantalisingly over her shoulder, making her shudder delicately and causing everything primitive within him to spike.

He forgot about friends *without* benefits as he held out the champagne flute. She took it from him slowly and in her eyes he saw heat battle with concern. 'How did it go?' she asked gently.

'It was fine.'

'You don't look fine. You look pretty grim. What happened?'

Her big heart was eager to soothe but he didn't want soothing, he wanted distracting.

'Be a friend and change the subject?'

For a moment he thought she was going to push it, but then, mercifully she looked around and then turned back to him to say, 'So I'm pretty sure that lady over there just told that dapper man with the moustache she belly-dances naked around the home!'

Jared's mouth dropped open as he looked to the man, who was currently bent double coughing, while the extremely overweight woman clapped him on the back.

Laughter erupted from him, 'You are so outrageous.'

She shrugged her shoulders and grinned, 'Sometimes the world calls for being a little outrageous. Stopped you thinking about your father, didn't it?' she smiled up at him with none-too-subtle dare in her eyes, 'Your turn.'

'To be outrageous?' Taking the glass out of her hands, he tipped it up to his lips and drank. 'You want to hear something outrageous?' he waited until she was looking at him expectantly and then leaned in to whisper, 'Lately, I've been thinking the "not sleeping with your best friend's sister" rule, pretty much stinks.'

Her lips opened to form a perfect "O". His skin pulled tight with need. And suddenly he wasn't so much regaining control as finding himself on the very edge of wanting to lose it with her. 'I do believe it's your turn.'

'Give me that,' she ordered, snatching the champagne glass back out of his hand and taking a gulp. 'What is the matter with you?'

'What? You told me to be outrageous. I thought I excelled myself. And I can pretty much guarantee that right now you're not thinking about my father either, are you?'

'You know, Jared, sometimes, as a friend you suck. But I guess that's okay.'

'Why, because, if we weren't friends, "bed" would be an option?'

'There is no "bed" with us. Only those things called rules. Brother/best friend rules. Employer/employee rules. *Business* rules-'

'I think you wish I'd be anything but businesslike with you tonight.' His eyes tracked her slow swallow, the hasty moistening of her lips. 'I think you wish that I'd find us somewhere private and turn you around and slowly untie that bow that seems to be all that's holding that dress up and—'

'Hey! Game over!' Mortified, she stared at his chest, unable to meet his eyes lest he saw the lust, the hurt, and the confusion… the whole gamut of emotions rushing through her.

Things really hadn't gone well with his father, and what, she was handy? Well didn't that make her feel all rosy? Except, disgustingly, it did. He'd only to look at her with those hooded green eyes and tell her she kissed like an angel. Hugging her arms to herself she forced a little volume into her voice. 'Congratulations on getting me to want exactly what you're offering.'

She saw the light of success enter his eyes and almost hated him for it. 'But believe me when I tell you how much I respect the fact that *want* doesn't always *get*.'

Oh, he didn't like that, did he? Judging from the way his jaw set granite-hard. Well tough. She had every right to protect herself. Things were changing between them and she felt the familiar stirrings of a panic she'd learnt to keep at bay by refusing to think ahead. Jared may well come under the heading of "want" but she was very afraid he could also come under the heading of "need". And that just wouldn't work for her.

His silence and intense regard spoke volumes. As if he knew the longer he spun his silence out the more she'd feel she was losing ground. Anticipation wended its way across each and every nerve-ending in her body. She willed herself not to sway towards him. 'You might want to have a little chat with yourself. Figure out what you really want from me. I thought I was supposed to be your Personal Assistant. But either way I'll tell you what I won't be. I won't be your Latest Limpet, Jared. And I won't be used as a way of avoiding the fall-out when things go off-plan for you. No matter how much I might want your hands and mouth on me.'

Chapter Four

'Amanda!'

Jared's roaring of/her name, being the umpteenth one of the morning, no longer had the power to shred her nerves. Instead she raised her eyes to the ceiling seeking patience while her hands paused over her keyboard. There was no need for her to respond. He'd be shouting for what he wanted in five, four, three, two—

'Where the hell is that breakdown you promised me thirty minutes ago?'

She breathed. Pressed 'print' and got up to walk over to the printer. Turning to put the sheaf of paper in a folder she found him filling the doorway between their connecting offices.

'I have it right here,' she said, tapping the folder against her palm. He just stood where he was, folded his arms and leaned against the door frame.

She pursed her lips and prayed again for patience. He was going to make her walk right over and place it in his hands? Fine; if he wanted to be that petty. Like the constant bellowing hadn't been clue number one to the fact he was still angry with her for saying what she had said and then promptly running out on him the other night.

She walked slowly towards him, demanding her body not to respond to the way his eyes drifted insolently to her hips before slowly sweeping back up the length of her.

She hated this silent war of seduction he seemed set on. Mostly because she suspected it would end when she found herself admitting she wanted him again. Not with him following through. It felt like a punishment disproportionate to the crime. 'Jared. I—'

He raised his eyebrow and all she could do was stand in front of him, the report occupying the space between them.

'Nothing,' she said, stopping short of clearing her throat. 'Do you need me for anything else?'

His eyes narrowed a fraction as if accusing her of deliberately making her question sound like more of a plea. 'What else could I possibly need you for?'

She felt the stab of hurt. They stared at one another, each from their own square foot of No Man's Land, fighting to find their balance whilst the ground constantly shifted under them.

'In that case, I have a lunch date.' She turned to go.

His hand shot out, and as if realising touching her wasn't a good idea, he left it hovering briefly in mid-air before reaching out for the report she was still holding.

'Who with?' he asked, deceptively soft in tone.

She was sorely tempted to give him a man's name. But then, what would that matter to him? 'Nora's taking me to a bakery that just opened.'

'She tell you that was my old motorbike she rode you home on the other night?'

'It was?' The smile came automatically. She and his sister must have looked quite the sight, long gowns tucked up high around their thighs as they'd sped off into the distance, the misty night air obscuring the outraged expressions upon the guests milling about outside.

For Amanda's part, she'd never been so glad of the offer of a lift in her life. When she'd run out on Jared she'd had no idea where she was going, only that she had to get away. She had been certain that if she'd stayed after her stupid admission about wanting him,

47

the combination of his potent sophistication and the plain old-fashioned lust he invoked would wrap itself around her and have her succumbing to anything he might have suggested. He'd been in a dangerous mood and she'd found that secretly thrilling. There was something about Jared that made a woman want to forget the consequences. Luckily she'd remembered just in time that she'd been ruled by or dictated to by consequences for most of her life.

And so she'd run.

It was too late to tell him now that she was sorry she had. That if she'd been a little braver, she had worked out that staying would have eventually forced him to admit he didn't really want her. He just wanted an escape. She figured hearing that would have put everything back into perspective. Certainly it would have helped slam the lid shut on all the want oozing out.

And perhaps if he'd been able to talk to her about how meeting his father had gone, she and everyone else in his vicinity wouldn't have had to endure the bear with a sore head act that he was currently refusing to drop.

'You know I don't think that was the first time your sister's taken that bike out for a spin. Maybe she's been looking after it until its original owner came back for it?'

Jared remained silent, although she thought she detected a brief expression of pleasure. But then he ruined it with, 'Be careful at lunch.'

'What's that supposed to mean?'

'It means you should ask yourself why Nora might be so intent on cultivating a friendship with you.'

'It couldn't be because my friendship is worth cultivating then?'

'Remember your loyalties, regardless of the fact that she's my sister, her first priority is saving this company.'

'Maybe that should be your first priority as well,' she tossed back.

'If she thinks she can get to me through you,' he stopped and unfolded his arms, 'if you think you can get to me through her—'

'Oh will you please get over yourself already. Nobody is going through anybody to get to anybody.'

He took a deep breath, as if doing so would imbue him with patience. 'You know the first rule of business is: don't antagonise the boss.' He stepped away and added, 'You'd better eat well at lunch. We're going to be working late tonight.'

'As in working late saving the company?'

That sexy side-smile of his came out to play. 'Amanda, how are you ever going to learn the second rule of business if you refuse to adhere to the first?'

'I guess that would depend on what the second rule is?'

'Second rule is: don't flirt with the boss.'

Her own smile, the one that had been so ready to spread across her face remained locked away. Just as soon as she got past wanting him, she'd start working on not doing that. She had to. His friendship was too important.

'You can have one hour. That's all I can spare you for.'

She sighed inwardly and turned and walked over to her desk to pick up her bag.

'Wait, are you meeting with Sephy too?'

'As it happens.'

'Then hang on. You can give her something to give to Daisy, for me.'

Intrigued, she followed him into his office, stopping abruptly when she found him hunched down in front of an enormous wooden dolls house.

'In retrospect, this might be a little large for you to carry.'

She burst into laughter, breaking the tension. 'You think?'

He looked up at her with a sheepish expression on his face. 'Also, I'm not sure how to wrap it.'

Her heart kicked painfully against her chest. Instead of their push-pulling at each other she should remember the stress he was under and try to make things easier on him. He had to be constantly walking into all those invisible boundaries that most siblings navigated with ease because of their shared history. His

49

map was ten years out of date and covered in unchartered territory. Should he attempt to reform old relationships, or try to make new ones with his sisters? How much did they want him in their lives? How much did he want to be in theirs?

'It's really beautiful.' She walked over and knelt down, stretching out a finger she ran it over the tiny roof tiles. 'Daisy will love it.'

'It's not too much?'

'Are you serious?' She caught the faint trace of uncertainty, the blush across his cheekbones and realised he was. It truly wasn't fair to be so hot *and* so adorable.

'What if she already has one?' he asked.

'So then she'll be starting her own King property portfolio.' She could tell he hated not knowing all of this already. 'You want me to run this by Sephy for you?'

He tilted his head to stare at the doll's house. She could see him running the angles. 'That would be...good. Thanks.'

'Perhaps you should invite your sisters over for a dinner? Get to know each other a little. Catch up. Find that common ground again. It doesn't have to be about business.'

He poked his finger through the doll's house front door to pull it shut. 'It's not that simple. Think they'll still want to chat through old times when I tell them that after Christmas KPC is finished?'

'It's that bad?'

'It's not good.' He ran his hand through his hair in frustration. 'Damn it, this is supposed to be their heritage.'

'Hey, it's your heritage too. You can find a way to make it work. I know you can.'

'KPC will *never* be my heritage.' He ran a hand through his hair and stood up. 'Forget it. You'd better be getting to lunch.'

Forcing herself to her knees she attempted to inject some lightness into her voice. 'I guess you're right. My boss is a slave-driver. In female-time one hour doesn't even cover a conversation about shoes.'

Amanda pushed her empty bowl of soup to one side feeling exhausted. She was under a very slick, very well-choreographed two-pronged attack. Operation 'what-has-our-brother-been up-to-for-the-last-ten-years' was being carried out with the stealth and vigour of a black-ops mission. She was feeling decidedly ambushed.

In the spirit of open communication, she was tempted to lead by example. But regardless of how much she was beginning to like his sisters, her loyalty was first and foremost to Jared and it wouldn't be right to drill them about his younger self. Instead she found herself couching questions in relation to how things had affected them.

'It must have been hard for you both when you realised he wasn't coming back?' she carefully asked.

'Actually what I mostly felt was guilt.' Nora said, fiddling with the handle of her coffee cup. 'It coincided with me thinking seriously for the first time about my career and what I'd decided upon was KPC.' She looked at Amanda as if expecting to see distaste. But Amanda was more interested in the fact that Nora had been able to plan out her life from such a young age and stick to it so unswervingly. 'Without Jared,' Nora continued, 'well, let's just say, it was far easier to get noticed. Dad poured all of his energy into a willing recipient. I was fast-tracked through the business. It took me a long time to stop feeling guilty about that. Now, I feel guilty it's taken me the best part of eighteen months since Dad's retirement to work out the state the company is really in.' She looked around her and lowered her voice. 'If the press get wind of his health, and the state of the business, before we're in a position to disclose our future—'

Amanda leant over and placed her hand on top of Nora's. 'Now is not the time to talk about this. This is exactly the kind of conversation you should be having with Jared. I know it must be hard—you feel like you hardly know him, like you're leaving yourself exposed. But talk to him, okay?'

Nora thought for a long while before nodding her head

51

infinitesimally and Amanda smiled. She'd seen Jared do that exact same thing. It was such a shame these three didn't know each other as well as they should. If they could come together on this she could imagine a bond that would never break, no matter the distance between them.

'I was a lot younger when Jared left,' Sephy mused. 'I guess I didn't ever really believe he wasn't coming back until he didn't. As a family it was never discussed. And so the questions built until finally I was forced to reach my own conclusion. Jared and father are too different. Being the eldest, Jared got to push the boundaries first, paving the way for the two of us to get away with much more. I think at some point he overstepped what father was prepared to put up with. He had a different group of friends that final year and I think Dad tried to stop him seeing them, Jared resented it so he just upped and left.'

Amanda held her tongue. True, she hadn't known Jared back then, but she could never reconcile the Jared she knew with the type of person he had said he had been. It made her more certain than ever that the three of them needed to get together and really talk about the past.

She knew better than most what it felt like living with unanswered questions – how you had to force yourself to live every day, *for* the day, or those questions ate away at you. It had taken her a long time after her parents' passing to realise that living for the day was key to keeping sane and surviving.

But the Kings had a choice. She wanted to tell them that having been presented with the chance, there was something to be said for asking the difficult questions and demanding answers to them, before the opportunity was taken from you.

'Do you have brothers or sisters?' Sephy asked.

'I have an older brother Mikey. He's a paraplegic.'

'Oh, that must be tough. What happened to him?'

'He was in a construction site accident.' She played it down because they didn't need to hear that Jared carried a burden of guilt upon his shoulders simply for asking Mikey to cover his shift that day while he scouted for business premises. Besides, there was a hell of a lot more to her brother than him being in a wheelchair. 'Actually, that only happened a few years ago. He's now a lawyer and has just got engaged to Jared's PA Janey.'

'I thought you were Jared's PA?' Sephy queried.

Amanda's heart skittered to a stop. Busted! 'Well, yes, I am—his other one.'

The two sisters exchanged a look.

'Told you,' Nora claimed, looking at her sister.

'Told her what?' Amanda asked.

'That she didn't think our brother would be kissing an employee in quite the way he did or that an employee would be kissing her boss back in quite the way you did, either.'

Faced with two incredibly polite, yet altogether too-knowing expressions, she found herself saying, 'I guess mostly what we are is friends.'

'Hate to tell you this,' Sephy said again, 'but friends don't usually kiss each other in that way either.'

'Tell me something I don't know,' said Amanda under her breath.

***

In the confines of their shared apartment, Amanda's quiet husky voice danced along the outer edges of Jared's consciousness.

'…so I'm probably doing something wrong, but every time I run the figures for the Butler project I come out with a saving of 1.9 million where they only have 1.1 million showing.'

'What?' Jared looked up with a frown, having only caught the last part of the sentence.

'Like I said, I'm probably doing something wrong.'

Jared winced at Amanda's choice of words. What it came down to, was that Amanda was doing everything right. That was the problem. That was *his* problem at least. She was able to distract him in a heartbeat.

'Let me take a look,' he said, trying to divert his thoughts back to the work at hand.

The report whizzed across the polished glossy surface of the dining room table as Amanda pulled another file from the pile to her left and reached for a takeout carton on her right.

He attempted to run the figures in his head.

Suggesting they work from the apartment had to rank right up there on what had been, until now, a very short list of bad ideas. As the soft lighting cast an intimate shadow over the proceedings he was vitally aware of Amanda and the fact that there were two bedrooms down the hall. Dragging the file towards him had him realising the hard smooth surface of the table provided another tantalising option. As if sensing his thoughts, Amanda groaned. He looked up and promptly lost his place. She was simply enjoying the food. Her phenomenal chopstick action had him mentally adding suggesting they get Chinese takeout to his growing list of bad ideas.

It was impossible not to continue watching as she placed another morsel into her mouth, the chopsticks serving to remind him of the first time she'd slanted her lips so softly and sexily across his. Inevitably that led to reminiscing about the other kisses they'd shared, all the while the voice on his shoulder taunted him for not running columns of figures.

She'd admitted to wanting his mouth and hands on her, yet, seemingly, she was still managing to hold onto her sanity. He was afraid her words had started the downward slide to him losing his. A tiny spark of an idea at the back of his mind was beginning to take hold and he was worried that if he examined that idea too closely, the next thing he'd be telling himself would be that it was perfectly permissible to explore the red-hot sizzling heat between them.

And after proper consideration he knew without doubt that it would be only a small step from exploring that heat to wanting to sate himself in it to its fullest, deepest sense; repeatedly.

Blinking he forced himself to run the numbers on the page before him.

'You're right about the saving. Better phone Nora first thing in the morning and set up a meeting between her and Frank from finance.'

'What about the project manager? Shouldn't he be in on it too?'

'Good thinking, but hold off until we've run the figures on all the other projects in development. Start with the ones with the same project manager. This might be a one-off so let's double-check before we get ahead of ourselves. If there's a pattern she's going to have to make sweeping changes and the board will fight her every step of the way using the excuse that she should have discovered this earlier. They've been disinclined to allow her any freedom to try new things. Her instincts are good but she's been too reluctant to act quickly, I suspect out of respect for them.'

'But it can't be as easy as finding and reapportioning a few extra million pounds, can it?'

'No. But it's a start.'

He watched the smile spread across her face. 'Now don't go getting ideas.'

'Who? Me?'

'Yes, you.'

There was still a smile on her face as she opened up the next file. She read a few pages and glanced up unexpectedly and he hated that it was to catch him still watching her.

'You can ask me, you know,' she said softly.

'Ask you what?'

'How lunch went.'

Jared reached for some food and chewed slowly. Thoroughly. And damned if she didn't just sit there patiently waiting for him to ask the very question he had sworn to himself he wouldn't.

'Talk about more than shoes, did you?'

'Daisy would love a doll's house from her Uncle Jared.'

Steady, he cautioned, deliberately quashing the quick, deep, spark of satisfaction her words brought. He hadn't returned to slip back into the family dynamic. He hadn't come back to shut KPC down either, not having been exposed to Nora's hard work and Sephy and her daughter Daisy. No, now it was a matter of showing his father he could reset KPC's future and leave again without it leaving any mark on him whatsoever.

Amanda got up and walked over to the kitchen area, returning with a bottle of red wine and two glasses. Pouring with a slightly unsteady hand she passed him one and took a slow sip from her own glass.

'Your father has an appointment with the specialist next week.' She took another sip and raised her eyes to his. 'The news isn't expected to be good.'

Jared didn't know the correct way to respond. He didn't know what to do with all the roiling anger, frustration and sense of loss. It couldn't possibly be grief he was starting to feel, could it?

'Sephy's planning on inviting us to dinner at the house the night before the appointment. She thinks it would be the perfect time to give Daisy the doll's house. Take everyone's mind off everything.'

His heart paused mid-beat. 'That's absolutely out of the question.' He couldn't be responsible for helping make everything better, he'd been away for ten years and was barely entitled to set foot inside the house.

'I had a feeling you'd say that.'

Jared's heart started beating again.

'So I accepted on your behalf.'

As his heartbeat stuttered again, Jared could think of other more pleasurable ways of ensuring his heart got a good workout. Taking a healthy swallow of wine, he put the glass out of his way and said, 'Well you can use your newfound friendship with my sisters to *un*-accept on our behalf.'

'Wow. I never had you down for a coward.'

Now his heart slowed to a heavy thud. 'Be very careful, Amanda.'

'Maybe I shouldn't have told you. If I'd waited until the invite you wouldn't have had time to plan your escape route.'

He leant back in his chair, willing each and every muscle in his face to relax; willing his heart-rate to remain steady. If she wanted to think the worst of him, what did he care? He was answerable to no one from the moment his father had believed business rivals over his own son and had cut him from the family tree like a canker. But perhaps he should be thanking his father. He'd learnt a valuable lesson, after all. Shutting down his reactions remained one of the strongest weapons in his arsenal and he'd earned the right to use it.

The fact that Amanda appraised him without fear had him admiring her for it, even as he steeled himself against letting her in.

'Careful, Jared, you might be asked to react to something other than business—better avoid going instead.'

'I can separate family and business.'

'No you can't.'

'Amanda. I can. Now, have you seen last year's annual report?'

Amanda laughed. 'That's it? That's your way of dealing with it? By ignoring the bits you don't want to deal with. Ignorance is bliss, huh Jared?'

God, as he kept his features deliberately schooled and began to look for the file himself he really hoped the bravado in her voice was false. 'The file?' he prompted.

He felt her get up from the table and walk around to him. With great care she put down her wine glass and took the last step needed to be standing within touching distance. Tucking her hair slowly behind her ear she leant over him, her breast maybe a millimetre from his shoulder as she reached across him.

His breath stilled against her cheek as he vowed dizzily that he could go without breathing in her scent for as long as she could tease him. Told himself he had enough control to cover her impulsiveness—and then some.

She deliberately pulled the wrong folder from the pile and,

placing it in front of him, turned the fraction needed to whisper directly in his ear, 'This what you want?'

He watched as her hand slowly stroked over the file and he went rock hard. Without thought he rose swiftly to turn and effectively trap her between himself and the table. 'It isn't. But then you know that don't you?' His words vibrated in the air as he lowered his head to watch the lust and irritation he was responsible for creating battle alongside each other on her beautiful face. He could practically hear her heart fluttering as he stood over her. He closed his eyes against the thrill of it and then forced them open to peer over her shoulder.

'Ah, there it is,' he managed to get out, as he picked up the annual report and held it in front of her. She reached out and curled shaking fingertips over the edge of it, lowering it so that he got an eyeful of pique and sexual arousal. The heady combination nearly undid him.

'It's late. You should get some sleep before tomorrow,' he said quietly.

'Careful, Jared. You might have to deal with me. Better shut me out instead.'

Pride had him stating, 'If I wanted to I could deal with you very well.'

'As it happens I think we could deal with each other very well.' Her head tipped to the side as she considered him. 'Maybe we should try and deal with that properly.'

'What are you suggesting, exactly?'

She dragged in a breath and his eyes lowered to the column of her throat. Testing himself, he let himself wonder what her skin would taste like at the base, where her pulse jumped with life.

Control, he cautioned as he moved his gaze back up to her face and watched her eyes go glassy.

'Oh I don't know—you probably wouldn't entertain any idea of mine unless it was on some sort of plan.'

'Interesting concept. Is that really you, though? Producing a detailed, thorough, plan?'

'I suppose you'd want bullet points.'

'Oh, I'd definitely want bullet points.'

'You really don't think I could do it, do you?'

'What?' He stepped back to get a better angle on reading her. 'Produce a list of pros and cons as to why we should stop what we're doing? Of course I do.'

'No, you don't think I could produce a written seduction plan.'

'Don't be silly.' The thought of Amanda seducing him... God help him, it wouldn't take much. He didn't get why he was allowing them both to play with fire like this. Was it London? Was being back here reminding him too much of his risk-taking maverick days, where he hadn't stopped to think about consequences, because the arrogance of youth made him think he could handle any that arose after? Or was it to avoid having to think about his father? Or was it that the statute of limitations on not thinking about Amanda as anything other than a friend had simply run out?

'Why not? Why don't you think I could do it?' she asked.

'You're being ridiculous.'

'Am I?'

'You know why this can't happen. What do you think Mikey would say?'

'If you can separate your family from this, then separate my family from it as well.'

'It's completely different and you know it. I shouldn't need to explain the trust Mikey has placed in me. And what the hell happened to "want doesn't always get"?'

'Maybe I've changed my mind. Maybe I figure it's worth it. Maybe I figure you're worth it.'

He reared back. 'Well, I'm not. You can get that out of your head right now. Say we stopped thinking and started acting. Say I lifted you onto this table and we had the hottest sex of our lives on it. What then?'

He watched fascinated as she leaned back on the table, hands braced behind her in a classic pose of submission and he actually found himself taking a step towards her before he could check himself.

'Well, if you're promising the hottest sex of our lives, I say that then, we would probably do it again.'

'Jesus.'

'And again.'

This wasn't a joke. It suddenly became imperative to shut this down. 'My point is you actually know me Amanda. Put everything you know about me and women into your thinking and then picture you in their place a month down the line. Remember what you said about having no wish to become my Latest Limpet and hold yourself to it. Because, let's face it, who would answer my Code Red if you were?'

'Do you have any idea how arrogant you sound?'

'Good. I hear arrogance is a real turn-off.'

'So to clarify—you don't think I could write a successful seduction plan because..?'

'Because in order to come up with a successful plan in the first place you'd have to sit down and actually think everything through. And if you want to put the responsibility back on me, because you think you wouldn't be able to do all that, then it's because when it comes to my best friend's little sister you can bet I'm always going to be risk-averse. We're friends. That's all.'

And God help him if she saw any of that as a challenge to try her hand at planning for him to become anything else.

Chapter Five

She'd take him to dinner and order every aphrodisiac on the menu. No, even better, she'd simply wait for him to come back from work. She'd be lying on the very table he'd mentioned having the hottest sex of their lives on, dressed only in one of his beautifully tailored, pure-white, buttoned-up work-shirts and a pair of killer heels. She'd leave the first three buttons undone, maybe have it falling open over one shoulder. He'd stand transfixed just inside the door, broodingly silent, every ounce of hot muscle going hard with need. And when she smiled and beckoned to him he'd hesitate only a moment before walking slowly towards her, drinking her in with his eyes. He'd lean down and without words slide his palms up and over her silky thighs. He'd swing her around on the polished tabletop and slowly, oh so slowly, push open her legs to stand between them. She'd lean back on her elbows, watching him through heavy eyes as his large capable hands moved to her waist to grip roughly and drag her the last vital distance needed to bring her into contact with his erection.

Amanda writhed against the smooth cotton sheets, opened her eyes and muttering a few choice words under her breath, turned over, grabbed one of the four pillows and threw it clear across the room, where it landed in a decidedly unsatisfying silent heap just short of the wall.

She glared up at the chandelier hanging from the bedroom ceiling. She absolutely, positively, needed to start asserting some self-discipline.

Fantasising about seducing Jared King? Very. Bad. Idea. What had started out as a 'what could it hurt to think about?' indulgence was fast-approaching her secret addiction.

She bit her lip at the delicious thought of testing that famous control of his. Bit down a little harder at the thought of Jared losing all that famous control. With her. *Because* of her.

Disgusted with the lack of her own self-control she plumped her remaining pillows and turned over again. She was so not going down this road. She was here to kick-start her life. Not give either of them a problem that followed them back to New York.

She closed her eyes and tried emptying her mind of all thought. Ever since joking about coming up with the stupid seduction plan, it had been virtually all she could think about. It meant she spent a large portion of her day and night feeling edgy and unfulfilled. She wasn't pleased to have her needs and wants highlighted like nothing else in a long, long time.

And she wanted Jared King. Big Time.

Embarrassingly, after their conversation, or rather, the lecture she'd had to endure the other night, it was as though he feared he couldn't trust her because for days now he'd gone out of his way not to accidentally touch her. He barely breathed when she passed him reports or reached over to replace his coffee. Did he think she didn't notice his subtle shuffle away from her as they stood side by side in the lift each morning, or the way he stayed on at work each evening, dismissing her back to the apartment while he worked late into the night.

What did he think she was going to do, jump him and proudly label it a successful seduction?

She huffed.

Somehow she didn't see sleep in her immediate future.

Maybe a drink would help.

Getting out of bed, she fumbled for her robe and dragged it on as she padded out into the living area. Halfway across the room she froze, her toes curling into the deep pile carpet.

Jared was sitting at the dining-room table, lazily watching her. A serious onset of the tingles worked her over from head to toe. No fair.

From her frozen position she took in the laptop and the half-drunk glass of wine.

For Heaven's sake, he must have been there all the while she'd been...

Double no-fair!

Before she could check herself her hands came up to secure the belt of her robe.

His cool, clear, green eyes lowered to the now exceptionally tight knot at her waist before slowly making their way back up to her face and even though his expression revealed nothing, she could swear his eyes had burned just a little brighter.

She tried clearing her throat without calling attention to the fact that standing there under his totally-in-command-of-himself gaze, she was finding it difficult not to blush, fidget and generally give the impression of wanting to fling herself at him. 'Sorry, I didn't realise you were back.'

Although why she was apologising, damn-straight it wasn't because she was practically naked under her bathrobe or anything. Squaring her shoulders she added, 'I was just about to get a drink.'

His eyes raked over her once more. 'You might want to put some clothes on first.'

The quiet, intense instruction containing the note of censure irked. 'Just to get a drink? I don't think so.'

His gaze narrowed slightly and she was vitally aware of his silent scrutiny as she walked over to the breakfast bar to switch the kettle on. A shiver of excitement danced down her spine and she racked her brain to come up with some small talk to break the tension.

But—nope; she had nothing. As the kettle slowly boiled she

risked a proper look at him. His attention had gone back to his work. His fingers stroked competently over the keyboard but as she studied his face she could see the fatigue. She knew he'd been working on a rescue package for KPC that had seen him locked in meetings with Nora for days. She and Nora's personal assistant had been allowed in at the tail end to help with collating all the relevant information. Jared had continued to work on the presentation while waiting for word that Nora had persuaded the board to hear him out. She knew it had been a difficult negotiation on his sister's part. If Jared knew his sister had ended up playing the family angle he hadn't let that affect his output. In the end, probably out of curiosity, the board had relented and a meeting had been convened for the following morning.

She had no doubt Jared worked hours like this throughout the running of his own company, but surely at some point he would need to rest, if only so that tomorrow he could perform to his best. 'You look exhausted,' she found herself saying, 'Maybe you should give work a rest for tonight.'

'Why? Have you something else in mind for me to do?'

Tongues of heat licked their way over her stomach. 'No. I mean,' this was ridiculous, unsure whether he was wired because of the task ahead or because of what had been happening between them, Amanda elected for trying to smooth things over, 'Jared, at some point we need to make the effort to relax around each other again. I got the message loud and clear the other night. Everything's back in perspective, you don't have to worry.'

He was silent for a moment before he did that head-tipping thing of his. 'So, your coming out here in nothing but that humungous fluffy white robe isn't an attempt to seduce me, then?'

For sheer effrontery she doubted he could be beaten. 'I just got through telling you,' she said exasperated and then stopped; caught the edge of humour in his voice and backed down a little. 'Fluffy white robes do it for you, do they?'

'The bigger the better.'

'Note to self,' she automatically flirted back.

This was better, if there had to be flirting, and now that she considered it, there had always been mild flirting between the two of them, it should definitely err more on the humorous and friendly banter level; not deeper. Deeper was dangerous. And just to make absolutely sure there was no suggestion of deeper, she said, 'I guess we both freaked each other out a little the other night. Why don't we leave it at that and agree to move on?'

She thought she detected a glimmer of disappointment in his eyes. Had to be wishful thinking on her part, didn't it?

'Kettle's boiled,' he observed when she lapsed back into silence.

'Oh.' Turning around she stepped over to one of the high kitchen cupboards to reach for the tea. Damn. 'Could you reach the herbal tea for me?'

Jared smiled and rose from his chair. He stepped in beside her to reach for the carton and as he brought the tea down to rest on the counter unit beside them she belatedly realised she should have moved out of his way. Her eyes fixated on his large beautiful hands and all she could think about was what they would feel like sliding up the backs of her thighs to cup her buttocks and gently squeeze. She swallowed and tried to move.

The atmosphere turned sultry as Jared, seemingly able to read her thoughts, stared silently down at her.

Just like that, both of them seemed hot and needy and tempted. Neither of them seemed at all freaked out.

She wondered what he'd do if she reached her hand out to stroke over the top button of his shirt—what he'd do if she looked up at him while she did, her eyes full of intent.

What if he stared back at her, waiting for her to fulfil the intent she promised with her eyes. What if the promise she saw mirrored in his eyes was so powerful, so overwhelming, it claimed not only her body but also her soul.

The realisation of which was enough to *actually* freak her out. This wasn't going to go away. Why wasn't it going away?

What could she do to make it go away?

She was going to have to come up with a proper plan to protect herself.

All of a sudden she felt like crying, because heaven knew coming up with any viable, sustainable plan was her kryptonite.

'Hey,' sensing the sudden change in her, Jared reached out a hand to tip up her chin and the physical contact, coupled with the concern she saw etched in his eyes was enough to garner movement. Taking a wobbly step backwards, she snagged the carton of tea off the side and turned to start preparing it.

In the continued silence she forced herself to glance at Jared and saw him standing with a frown on his face, hands shoved deep into his pockets. For once the shutters hadn't been deployed but still she wished she could fathom what was in his eyes. Wished she knew whether the frown was down to confusion over her behaviour, or confusion over his reaction.

She attempted a reassuring smile, but if anything, his confusion turned back to concern again.

'Why don't you give Mikey a ring?' he offered, clearing his throat slightly. 'You must be missing him and I'm sure he'd like to hear your impressions of London.'

Amanda dunked the herbal tea in and out of the cup. Oh Lord, his attempt to make everything better really had her worrying that tears were on the horizon. She forced the panic inside her back down into the special place she'd spent years creating and tried to tell herself she was being silly. There were bound to be a few wobbles as they both endeavoured to emphasise their friendship in favour of downplaying the awareness between them. Nothing was going to change between them, unless they let it. She should give herself some credit for just now pulling back from the brink the way she had. She could do this. Could continue doing this. It was all good.

'That sounds like a great idea, thanks.'

'Use my phone, if you like,' he said, indicating the one on the plush L-shaped sofa in front of one the large windows.

He moved to seat himself back down at the table, returning his attention to the laptop in front of him and after taking a sip of her tea she headed for the sofa and the phone.

She scrolled until she found her home number and dialled.

'Mikey?'

At the first sound of his, 'You don't phone, you don't email, what the hell's up with that?' she smiled, relaxed and pulled her knee up to rest her elbow on.

'You are such a grouch. Think Janey will still marry you when she clues in to your real disposition?'

There was a short silence and then she heard her brother's gruff, 'God, Manda Panda, I feel so bad for not telling you about the engagement from the get-go.'

His pet name for her had warmth flooding through her. 'Haven't we already gone over this? Save the apology for when the two of you swan off on honeymoon and I'm the one stuck having to return five of the six toasters you get given as wedding presents.'

'Speaking of which, London, pros and cons, please.'

'London as a honeymoon destination?' she glanced swiftly at Jared but he seemed ferociously focused on his work. 'Er, I haven't actually seen all that much of it yet. But, hey, the history, the architecture, the shopping, the food. What's not to like?'

'But is it romantic?'

'Romantic?' she swallowed realising that Jared had momentarily stopped typing. She would not look at him. 'Like I said I haven't seen all that much of it yet.' She took a breath when Jared resumed typing. 'Anyways, the very fact you'll be on your honeymoon will mean it's romantic. You could be anywhere.'

'True. So, is Jared treating you right?'

'Of course he is, idiot!' Interesting how a human voice could jump an octave in a nanosecond.

'No funny business?'

'Don't be crazy, Mikey.' Heat wended its way up her body,

suffusing her face as Jared's fingers once again stopped on the keyboard.

'And the work?'

'I think it's going well, haven't managed to screw anything up yet, anyway. When I get back home I'm going to be fierce in interviews. I'll have my own place, in an area my brother approves of, in no time.'

'About that—you know you don't have to move out.'

'Of course I do. I want to,' she added for good measure.

'I'll need to look the place over.'

'Yes, Dad,' she teased, 'it's not like I'll get any peace until I agree anyway.'

'Just so long as we're clear on that. Thanks for our engagement present by the way.'

'You're welcome.' Amanda had given them a framed photo she had taken of them at Jared's New Year's Eve party a couple of years ago. Janey had been sitting on Mikey's lap laughing up at him. Mikey had been smiling down at her, both of them caught in a private moment, completely oblivious to everyone else.

Amanda flashed back to the New Year's party she and Mikey had thrown to celebrate the changes in his life. She saw herself staring at the three-point plan she'd made on her phone and remembered her resolution to follow through. Funny how, in London, with Jared, all of that had shifted to the back of her mind as more and more Jared had started taking up the space at the forefront.

'You know,' Mikey said, 'it got Janey and me thinking that maybe you would like to do the photos for our wedding.'

Her heart skipped a beat. 'Er, the words "professional wedding photographer" need adding to your wedding file, like now.'

'Come on Manda Panda. You're just as good as any professional out there.'

'Mikey, you and Janey can afford to hire a real professional. Do it. You deserve to have the best photos you can possibly get.'

'But that's exactly why we want you. We'd be so much more

relaxed. You'd be able to get the candid shots that count; really capture the feel of the day. But, you know, you don't have to say "yes" right now. Take some time to think about it. Just know that, you know, given the choice, Janey and I choose you.'

Amanda pulled at the cotton covering her knee and closed her eyes as she felt the first fluttering of panic. Stupid. So stupid, not to have seen this coming.

'Alright,' she found herself answering, 'If it's what you both want. I guess I could—'

'That's great. Hey, Janey,' she listened to her brother talking excitedly to Janey in the background. Somehow she was going to have to find the time to start practising. Seriously read up on poses and portraiture and how to photograph weddings perfectly. Maybe, in the same way that some of the business skills she had studied at university had come back to her, her photography skills would too. She bit her lip. Why hadn't she taken the time to think, like Mikey had offered? Now she was committed to producing something other people would judge her on, with the added stress of making sure she didn't let her brother down. She plucked the piece of cotton clear out of the robe she was wearing and worried it with her fingers. This was way too big to wing. She was going to have to plan it all out properly.

Her hand crept up to her sternum and she began to rub gently. 'Mikey, I should be going. I'll email. Maybe send some photos of London.'

She heard his quick goodbye and dropped the phone back down onto the sofa.

The typing behind her had never resumed. Not wanting to acknowledge that, Amanda reached for her cup of tea and with shaking hands took a cautious sip.

'So you're going to be Mikey and Janey's official wedding photographer?' Jared said from behind her.

Damn. Amanda's eyes fluttered shut. 'It would seem so.'

'And do you actually want to do that for them?'

She opened her eyes, turned towards him and shrugged.

'You wouldn't rather be their guest and relax for the day?'

'Maybe I hadn't planned on this, but it's not like I wouldn't have my camera on me anyway.'

'Right.'

His tone said it all. She needed something to do. Catching sight of the offending article she reached for the camera and turned it on to play with it.

'Well, I'm certainly enlightened,' Jared continued, 'Who knew you were one of "them".'

She started flicking through some of the photos she'd taken. 'One of whom?'

'A real bona-fide people-pleaser.'

'Me?' her head shot up to look at him, 'Are you serious? I'm the weird one who abhors structure, remember? That hardly constitutes people-pleasing if you and my brother are to be believed.'

'Ah, but now I see that your very lack of a life makes you totally accessible. You swan around pretending to please absolutely no one but yourself and yet all the while you're busy moving heaven and earth to make sure you're available to please everybody else. All this "I don't need to follow a plan" nonsense is actually more about you making sure you're constantly available in case someone asks something of you. Tell me, what happens if you're not available?'

'I haven't a clue what you're talking about.' The door to that special room within her started rattling, the panic threatening to break out.

'Yes you have. How many times have you ditched your plans to suit someone else's needs?'

'Everyone does that for family and friends.'

'Everyone doesn't. Not all the time, at any rate. What would you have done if Mikey had said he needed you in New York when I said I needed you here?'

Amanda licked her lips. It would have tested her. But she'd have found a way to work out which option upset the apple-cart the least, gone with the one the Planning Gremlins were least likely to wreak havoc on.

She risked a look at him. Somehow she didn't think saying that out loud would help her sound in any way sane.

'You didn't really need *me* per se,' she said instead.

'I didn't ask anyone else to come to London with me.'

Her palms started sweating. 'I kind of thought you asked me here to salve your conscience.'

'But did you say yes simply to please me, or because it was what you really wanted to do?'

She listened intently to the whirr of the camera as she switched it off and stood up. She *wasn't* a slave to everyone's needs. She was perfectly capable of acting upon what she wanted. And what she wanted was for this conversation to be over. 'You know that herbal tea really did the trick. I think I'm tired enough to turn in now.'

She looked defiantly at Jared, daring him to say something more. He was focused on the camera in her hand and she could see that incredible mind of his processing.

'Did you even want to study business at university, or was that Mikey's idea?' he asked quietly.

So she'd dropped business to concentrate on photography a week before Mikey's accident. So what? What did any of it matter now anyway? Life happened. Plans changed. It wasn't a big deal. And if she didn't want to talk about this with him, she didn't have to.

'You're reading something into nothing. Goodnight, Jared.'

'Amanda?'

She paused in the corridor but couldn't turn around to face him.

'You know I asked you once if you were going to let fear rule you.' He stopped and the added quietly, 'I never had you down for a coward, either.'

Back in her room she paced. Okay, so, she may well be a coward. It was good that she was a coward, she thought as she fought the swirling emotions. Because if she wasn't a coward she'd be getting out the paper and pen and writing herself a seduction plan so brilliant, so powerful, he wouldn't know what hit him. That would show him. That would prove to him she had the courage to plan how to attain her own desires.

Didn't he understand? Didn't he get it? Of course she didn't want to let fear rule her life. Didn't she battle it every blessed day?

She sank down onto the bed as the reality that she'd been lying to herself slammed into her. She had stopped battling the fear a long time ago. Instead, she lived with the absolute acceptance that reaching out for what she wanted in life tended to ensure it was somehow snatched away from her. Had she ever had any real intention to push herself to follow through on those New Year resolutions? Was she really so defeatist?

She pressed a trembling hand to her stomach. That was awful, pitiful even. And to not even try to rise above it any more—that was worse than cowardly. That was downright apathetic. What would her parents, who had been so full of life, have to say about that? How could she squander what she had been given, biding her time, for what, exactly? It's not like she didn't know how precious life was.

She glanced down to her beloved camera and picked it up to switch back on. Flicking through the images she realised it wasn't all bad. Jared might have thought her agreeing to make a record of Mikey and Janey's big day was just another way of pleasing everyone else, but the reason her heart had skipped a beat was because she had recognised an opportunity. A great opportunity. And her first inclination hadn't been to hide but to grasp at it. Regardless of how certain she was that something would inevitably go wrong.

Well, she wasn't going to let herself back away this time. She was going to learn how to plan for every possible eventuality and make sure she had it covered, because there was no way she was letting herself down any more.

Ironically she probably had Jared to thank for her new perspective; if he hadn't taken her out of her comfort zone in the first place and exposed her to all his planning...

Her finger paused over a photograph she'd taken of him a few days before, his expression as usual inscrutable. She brought the camera closer so that she could study the screen but it didn't help. Glancing around she searched for the laptop he'd given her to work on. Fetching the leads to her camera she plugged the camera in and downloaded the photograph to her screen saver. Studying it she savoured the angles of his face, the unflappable, defiantly confident and powerful intelligence. Behind the eyes there were all sorts of thoughts going on as that brain of his constantly flexed its considerable muscle.

He was her very private portrait of sensuousness.

Maybe if she worked with him for long enough she'd absorb some of his ability to plan her way through life. Maybe she'd be so busy doing that it would distract her from wanting him with a fierceness that just wouldn't let go.

Sudden inspiration struck, and galvanised into action she settled herself onto the bed and opened up a fresh document. Buzzing with energy and with a secret smile on her face she typed: Seducing Jared King. The Plan.

Underlining it she began typing.

This was just for her, of course. A reward for not backing away from the photography deal she'd just made with her brother.

It was for practice.

It was for therapy.

For proving to no one but herself that she could figure all the angles and produce a well-thought-out plan.

She typed for hours, rearranging the pillows and propping herself up in bed with the comforter pulled around her when she got chilly.

In the 'why' section she examined the awareness between them and described the solution as perfect for getting it out of their systems so that they could return to New York as the friends they were supposed to be. Curiosity assuaged, urges sated.

In the 'where' section she went with a short essay on 'What happens in London stays in London'.

In the 'when' section she wrote one word: ASAP. Anticipation was so last year.

In the 'how' section she went to town, setting out in explicit detail exactly how she would go about seducing Jared. The words flowed easily, falling from the place where her imagination went untamed.

Yawning and flexing her fingers to un-cramp them she read through the plan one last time, pleased with her efforts. It was logical, thoughtful, creative and all-encompassing.

It was a shame it was never going to see the light of day.

As a final touch, before sleep claimed her, she made sure she bullet-pointed everything.

Chapter Six

'Amanda?'

Amanda's head shot up from the desk as Jared called her name.

'Did you get any sleep at all last night?' he asked from his office doorway.

'I'm totally fine,' she replied, faking it to the max. She passed a hand over her mouth, surreptitiously checking for dribble. It could only have been seconds that she'd actually been asleep for, right? How long had he been standing there, watching her? And, more to the point, what right did he have to be looking so darned fresh and *awake*?

Gingerly she rolled her head from side to side, wanting to stretch.

She would have to have had her personal epiphany on the eve of Big Presentation Day. She couldn't have had it another night, when he wouldn't be relying on her the next day.

Although, as if Jared would allow something as trivial as his Personal Assistant being found asleep at her desk to put a dent in his confidence. He looked pumped and eager to do battle and Amanda wondered if Nora was ready to see this side of him in her boardroom.

'If you need to go back to the apartment and try and get some sleep—'

She shook her head. 'Nice try but I am not leaving you today.'

'I'm sure I'd be able to cope. I don't expect you'll even be needed in the boardroom. In fact I just came out here to ask you to print out some hard copies of the presentation and put a backup copy of it on a pen drive. I can't remember whether the boardroom is wireless.'

'Base covering, huh?' Ha! Yet more proof she had what it took to develop one first-class plan. She had already backed up *her* plan on a pen drive first thing this morning when she'd switched on her laptop, only to find the document winking up at her, daring to be read again. Writing the plan had boosted her confidence and banished a few of her demons. If only she didn't feel so tired, she'd probably be able to do something with this glow inside of her. 'I'll start on the copies,' she offered instead.

'Knock, knock,' Nora said, poking her head around the door, 'all set?'

'Sure. Amanda's printing out some last-minute copies and I'm good to go.'

'Excellent.' Nora came all the way into the room. 'I can't begin to tell you what this will mean to me, Jared. To KPC, to father, if this works out,' she stopped and wiped nervous hands down her sides, 'I don't know how to thank you.'

Amanda hunted around for a pen drive, smothered yet another yawn, and promised herself the largest, strongest cup of coffee she could get her hands on, just as soon as both Nora and Jared were tucked safely away in the boardroom. She was feeling anxious enough for the both of them and coupled with the lack of sleep, was really beginning to feel quite wobbly.

'On a completely separate note,' she heard Jared's sister say as she began printing copies of the presentation, 'have you decided to accept Sephy's invitation to the house tonight?'

There was a short pause before Amanda heard Jared respond.

'About that, thank her for me, but I've decided my PA deserves a night out. She hasn't seen much of London yet and she's been working really hard.'

Abruptly stopping what she was doing and turning her head, Amanda looked at Jared and caught her breath. He had that determined look in his eyes, confident she wouldn't say anything to contradict him.

She looked to Nora and caught the slight pleading expression in her eyes.

'Er, I can go sight-seeing any old time,' she said, hoping her hands wouldn't shake as she started assembling the printouts into smart leather folders. 'I'm sure Daisy would love to get her hands on that doll's house you've got for her.'

Nora looked relieved as she turned to Jared. But Jared just continued to stare at Amanda. She licked her lips when she detected his disappointment. Had he really thought she'd go along with his plans? Plans that quite conveniently once again allowed him to back away from the olive branch his family appeared to be extending?

'Maybe I'll have it couriered over. Or,' he said turning to his sister, 'you could always take it with you tonight.'

Amanda watched Nora's face fall and wanted to help. It was obvious his sister didn't think she was in a position to push the invitation. It was virtually impossible to gain the upper hand with Jared, and Nora was thoroughly aware he was about to step into the boardroom for her. There was no way she would jeopardise that.

On the other hand, Amanda knew Jared better than his family. He could be pushed alright; he was big enough to fight his corner and had too much integrity to allow presenting to the board to become a bargaining chip. In fact, she was beginning to realise that half the time his plans went so smoothly it was simply because no one dared call him on them.

'Jared, you must have spent a lot of time choosing that gift,' she said softly, 'why not get the pleasure of seeing Daisy open it tonight. Join in the *family* celebration.'

'I will not confuse her like that. This presentation is going to go well and you and I are going to be on a plane headed back home by the end of the week. There won't be any Uncle Jared popping over for visits then, or taking her out to the zoo for the day. There will just be birthday presents and Christmas presents and thank-you letters exchanged.'

'But Jared, it doesn't have to be—'

'I don't believe I need to explain myself any further. Now, are those copies ready? Presentation backed up?'

Amanda silently passed him his laptop and pen drive. She'd pushed him as far as she could.

He popped the pen drive in his suit trouser pocket and reached a hand out for the folders. Quickly counting them he passed her several back. 'You've done too many extra.'

'Oh. Sorry,' she hadn't really been paying enough attention while she'd printed, collated and assembled. She clutched the extras to her chest as he and his sister made their way to the boardroom.

Breathing out slowly she glanced down at the warm leather folders in her hands. He was so confident about his plans that she opened up one of the folders, keen to read the presentation in its complete form for the first time. She expected to see KPC's logo and the project name cleanly stated on the cover page of the presentation.

Instead she saw a cover page that at its centre, in bold, magnificent, enormous font, clearly read:

Seducing Jared King. The Plan.

What the..?

Oh dear God, no.

No, no, no, no, no.

This could not be happening.

She shook her head violently in denial, refusing to believe she could have printed out her stupid seduction plan instead of Jared's presentation to the board. It wasn't possible. Wasn't. Wasn't. Wasn't.

She ran over to her desk. She didn't understand. Maybe it was just some sick joke her mind and eyes were playing on her because she was so tired.

She closed her eyes, counted to three and opened them to stare at the folders.

Seducing Jared King: The Plan... was the front page of all of them.

She flicked through each of the spare copies. Words like Licking, Stroking and Squeezing, jumped out at her as if they'd been written quadruple times the font size she'd actually used.

Oh God, she'd used the wrong pen drive. Printed out the wrong document.

A horrified, manic sort of giggle hiccupped out of her.

She was so beyond dead it wasn't even funny.

Suddenly she was off and sprinting to the bank of lifts that would zoom her up to the boardroom.

Bypassing the alarmed receptionist she put her hands on the double doors, yanked to open them and without pausing for breath or thought, stepped over the threshold.

She was met with stunned silence.

The sudden halting of forward momentum had the ground rushing up to meet her, making her stagger slightly.

Jared was up and out of his seat in a flash.

'What's the matter? Are you ill? Is it Mikey?' he asked, his voice an urgent whisper near her ear.

Numbly she shook her head. The consequences of her madly unprofessional entrance combined with the very real possibility that everyone in the room was about to read her most private fantasy rendered her, for the first time in living memory, mute.

'Amanda,' Nora said, rounding the huge beautiful oval teak conference table. 'I think I know why you're here.'

Amanda swung around to stare in desperation as Nora walked towards her, the pile of folders safely grasped in her hands. There was a strange rackety, laboured sound and gradually it dawned on her it was the sound of her drawing breath for the first time since she'd discovered what she'd done. She reached out her hand, eager to have the folders in her possession. Eager to take them, turn and run as far as her feet could take her, preferably to the end of the world, where she could fling them and herself over the edge.

Nora stopped in front of her and with a message in her eyes that Amanda was very afraid meant she'd be explaining herself in detail, very soon, conveyed to the rest of the room, 'I've mistakenly picked up the wrong files,' turning back to a red-faced Amanda, she said, 'I take it you realised and have kindly brought the correct versions, with you?'

Amanda wanted to fall on her knees and weep with gratitude. The minute she got out of here she was buying Nora the pair of shoes she'd seen her coveting in a boutique by the bakery the other day. But then Nora's question sank in and had her paling.

Of course she didn't have the correct versions. That would imply she was an efficient, practical, lateral-thinking, PA. When, of course, she was in fact plain old Amanda Gray, the one the Planning Gremlins used to sic their young on.

She should have known.

She'd made a plan and the plan had gone wrong. Never mind the plan was never meant to have seen the light of day. She'd gone ahead and done it and now look.

Tears gathered. You'd think by now, knowing how she usually faired with the whole planning malarkey, she'd have found the moxie to extricate herself from the scrapes she got herself into when everything went wrong. Instead, her inner reserves were giving her crying? How, exactly, was that supposed to help?

Jared took one look at the tear-gathering and advanced a step as if to protect her. She blinked with mortification, determined not to let him down in front of these people, who were today discussing the company's future.

Inhaling a shaky breath she side-stepped Jared, took the folders from Nora's hands and sent her a look that said 'I owe you my first-born'.

Walking around the table she stopped in front of Jared's laptop.

'Ladies and gentleman,' she said as professionally as she could,

'I'm Amanda Gray, Mr King's PA. I'm terribly sorry to interrupt but I won't be a moment. Mr King, if I could just check your pen drive? It's in your trouser pocket,' she brazened out when he raised an eyebrow at her as if she was mad.

Their silently conducted conversation had her interpreting his brook-no-argument expression as 'as soon as this meeting is over, you and I are going to be having ourselves a little talk, whereupon I get to the bottom of what's going down here.' Her silent reply went more along the lines of 'You really don't want to know what nearly went down here'.

He pulled out his pen drive and with shaking hands she took it from him and inserted it into the computer. She nearly fainted with relief as she located only KPC files, his presentation being the largest file and clearly marked.

She dragged in a breath. 'Okay. Mr King has the correct, most up-to-date version of the information he needs and I will leave you in his capable hands.' She sent a copy of the file to her laptop. 'I will be making hard copies of the presentation,' she broke off as out of the corner of her eye she saw Jared pick up one of the folders she'd put down. In her haze of panic, she wasn't sure, but she thought her hand actually left the keyboard to reach out and slap his hand away from it.

A nano-second later and her hand dangled uselessly in mid-air because it was too late. Jared had opened up the folder and was staring down at the cover page.

She really thought she might expire on the spot. As she dragged in a breath, she couldn't help wishing that she would. It would at least provide a solution to her having to actually deal with the most humiliating experience of her life.

She watched in morbid fascination as a dull flush appeared across his cheekbones. Continued to watch as he turned the first page and skimmed through it. He turned the second page and as if belatedly realising where he was, his head shot up to her. She found herself actually wanting, silently begging, for those famous shutters of his to slam into place so she wouldn't have to witness the look in his eyes that said that she'd written one hell of a plan, which was so beside the point.

With a strength she didn't know she possessed she dragged her eyes back to the other occupants in the boardroom. 'As I was saying,' she stopped, cleared her throat and tried again. 'I will make sure that hard copies of Mr King's presentation are delivered to you all. Apologies for the interruption and er, thank you for your patience.'

She gathered up the folders and steeling herself held her hand out for the copy in Jared's hands. Another ten seconds and she could high-tail it the hell out of here and begin her meltdown in private.

'I'll keep this copy, Miss Gray.'

Her mouth dropped open.

'Thank you. That will be all.'

Two hours had passed since Amanda had delivered the copies to the boardroom.

One hundred and twenty minutes and the only positive thing she could say about them was that all trace of tiredness had disappeared.

In fact she was possibly the most alert she had ever been. She was certainly hyper-sensitive to the ping of the lift.

She'd tried to work out what she would say to Jared when he invariably called her into his office to fire her. But being fired was the least of her concerns. She was more worried about the fact that *it* was now out there.

Maybe her best option was to treat *it* lightly. Except 'lightly' didn't seem to be a word she could get her brain around. She hit stumbling block after stumbling block as she tried examining the ramifications to Jared knowing she'd actually gone ahead and written down his own seduction. She'd never felt less emotionally light in her life.

Amongst the sirens and clanging bells going off in her head she distinctly heard the ping of the lift and Jared's quite unmistake-able baritone.

Oh Lord.

She stood up.

She sat down.

The voices came closer.

She rested her hands on the keyboard, brought up a fresh document and began typing utter gobbledygook.

Nora and Jared entered the room in unison.

'—you were brilliant, Jared. Absolutely brilliant.'

'I take it the meeting went well?' Amanda said, reaching to subtly close her document.

'The best,' Nora laughed. 'I'll let this one here tell you all about it. I'm straight back to my office to start work on those changes.'

Left alone in the office with Jared, Amanda figured she might as well get it over with.

'I'm sorry.' That didn't sound good enough. She licked her lips and tried again. 'I'm really sorry. I've behaved thoroughly unprofes-sionally. Typing something like that up on work property, worse, not paying enough attention this morning, so that I ended up printing it out. I feel sick when I think about the damage I could have done if those folders had been handed out at the meeting. It's to your credit that you were able to behave so well when faced with my thorough incompetence—'

'Amanda,' Jared interrupted.

'You don't have to say it. I completely understand. In fact, I fired myself.'

'You did, huh?'

She looked at him. He thought she was joking? 'Of course. Gross incompetence or misconduct or something isn't it? I'll have a look at flights back to New York in a minute.'

'Listen, I don't care what you look up outside of work hours but inside of them, how about you concentrate on your job instead?'

'But Jared, you must see—'

'I see a PA, who upon realising she had made a mistake, had the courage to walk into that meeting and attempt to sort it out.'

'Jared, it can't be that simple. You know what's in that folder.'

'Why can't it? No harm came of it.'

'No harm?' she stopped and considered. She supposed he hadn't actually read what she'd written, not in its explicit entirety anyway. She drew in breath, 'so are you going to let me have that back?' she asked, indicating the leather folder tucked under his arm.

'Certainly not. In fact, hold all my calls for me, will you?'

He made to get into his office but she was on her feet before him.

'Oh no way, you can't be serious?'

There was a damned twinkle in his eye, when he said, 'Amanda, you know me, I'm always serious.'

In a desperate bid to stop him she followed him to the connecting door between their offices. 'That's private property, hand it back,' she demanded. 'Please,' she begged when he simply stood staring at her. But even to her own ears, she sounded weak and feeble and utterly unconvinced by her bad-ass approach.

For one shining moment, it looked as though he was about to put an end to her torture and pass the folder back to her. But then he smiled. That ridiculously sexy side-smile of his. The exact one she'd responded to a couple of weeks before when this insanity between them had started spiralling out of control.

'As you point out, anything written on a work-supplied laptop, anything printed out on KPC stationery...'

Oh, she was so dead.

Again.

She tried to analyse what, exactly, the difference was between knowing someone had written something about you and knowing exactly what it was that had been written. She felt the wave of heat suffuse her body, felt her heart trip over itself. Yeah, him knowing the exact detail of what she had written was worse. Way, way worse. There would be nowhere to hide; no way of pretending she didn't badly want him. No way of pretending that she didn't want him to want *her*. Badly.

In fact, this was so bad she briefly considered going the whole hog and asking if she could read it to him herself.

Her eyes widened in shocked denial, as she realised that the tiniest part of her wanted to see what his reaction would be to reading about his own seduction by the hand of his very own, very personal, personal assistant.

Jared moved into his own office seemingly in slow motion, as if, were she a better person, she would be able to reach out and stop him. But before she could even begin to wonder how to do that, he was saying, 'I'll buzz you if I need you for anything,' and shutting the door firmly in her face.

She stood rooted to the spot.

He was in his office, right now reading what she'd written.

She didn't know what to do.

Walking to her desk, she sat down jerkily.

She stared unseeingly at her monitor before slowly reaching out to click on the mouse and deleting the gobbledegook on the document she'd opened earlier.

Placing her fingers on the keyboard she started typing: Oh My God, over and over again until gradually her breathing levelled out and some kind of thought process returned. Suddenly the words on the screen changed to: What would Jared do?

Her hands left the keyboard. That was a very good question. What *would* Jared do if the roles were reversed?

Of course he would probably have a plan and a back-up plan. And she could bet those indomitable shutters of his would play a large part.

She chewed down on her lip, her mind racing. And suddenly she loved the shutters.

The shutters would save her.

Jared put the folder down and pushed his chair back. He needed air. Running his finger around his shirt collar he decided it was high time offices went all retro and started storing nice decanters of brandy in them again. He could do with a drink. Hell, he could do with a shower. A cold shower.

For the first time in years he didn't know what to do next. He knew what he wanted to do... But that in no way meant that he should.

He frowned. The women he dated liked him being in control and specifically in control of their pleasure. It was how he liked it too. He wasn't used to a woman carefully plotting *his* pleasure in such incredible detail.

Unable to leave it alone, he picked up the folder to re-read what she'd written. It had him smiling in under a minute.

It had him hard in less.

Last night he'd called Amanda Gray a coward.

Her response had been to produce a plan so bold and beautiful, so tactically thrilling, so downright delicious... If the material wasn't of such a personal nature he'd be applauding her and calling her a worthy business opponent.

He was beginning to think that people-pleasing was her strongest weapon. She certainly seemed to know what would please him.

He shut the folder with a snap.

None of this was telling him what the hell he should be doing about her, her plan and his reaction to her and her plan.

Maybe there was nothing to worry about. Amanda was no coward, but surely now she knew that *he* knew about the plan, she wouldn't follow through on it. A good tactician would know the tables had turned.

A smile formed. She was mortified enough for the both of them. He should leave it alone. Pretend she'd never written it. Pretend he'd never read it. He pulled his chair back up to his desk and reached for the intercom.

That she made him wait annoyed him, but he let it pass. He was in control.

'Have a seat,' he said when she finally stepped into his office, closing the door firmly behind her.

He watched as she took the five steps necessary to reach the chair. She sat down and crossed her legs. He heard the soft whisper of silk on silk and was immediately transported to number fourteen on her "how" list.

He pulled a pad of paper towards him and casually wrote the word "control" in block capitals in the corner.

He looked up, wary of her calm, patient demeanour. He was more used to the way her emotions ran close to the surface and how they bubbled over with ease. It was one of the things about her that helped him stay in control.

'I was wrong to imply you didn't know what went into putting a plan together,' he said, by way of an opener, 'I apologise.'

'Thank you. I appreciate it.'

She appreciated it? That was it? 'You obviously put a lot of thought into it,' he added.

She seemed to weigh her words before saying, 'Jared, rather than discussing my skill in making a plan, oughtn't we actually be discussing what to do about what you've read?'

'Discussing..?'

'Alright then, you talk and I'll listen. You're in complete control of this situation.'

'And you're not?' Her newfound ability to remain so locked down, when she was usually the exact opposite, was starting to annoy the hell out of him.

'I meant in the sense that obviously it's now down to you to decide what to do about what you've read.'

'It's not to be a mutual decision then?'

Amanda laughed and the warm sound had him reaching out to draw a box around the word he'd written on the pad of paper.

'We both know how important it is to you that you own and control your decisions. I guess what I've worked out is that ultimately you won't let what you've just read affect our friendship. Ultimately, you're going to be the bigger, better person. It's who you are.'

He sat there stunned. God, but she made him want to be that other person. The one who swept her off her feet, laid her down on his desk and satisfied the both of them without thought to consequences.

'Shall I be getting back to work, then?' she asked after what she obviously considered a suitable pause.

'Perhaps you should.'

She'd surprised him for the second time that day. He watched as she rose from her chair and smoothed her skirt down with her hands.

Let her go, let it go, it's the right thing to do. You know it. She knows it.

He watched her open the door.

He didn't like that he was unable to surprise her.

'Amanda?'

'Yes?'

'Let my sisters know we'll be popping by the house tonight, after all.'

'We will?'

For the first time he saw a fraction of all that tightly leashed emotion leak out. 'Mmmn. Be sure to mention we won't be staying for long, though.'

'We won't?'

'No. We have plans after.'

'Plans?'

'Specifically, this plan,' and he picked up the leather folder and grinned.

He had to admit, as he caught her double blink, she rallied well. His heart hitched as he watched her calmly step back over the threshold once more and firmly shut the door behind her, before turning to look at him.

'What has going to see your family got to do with,' she waved her hand about before pointing to the plan, 'that?'

'It doesn't really. But, out of the two of us, you seem to be the only one who speaks "family" and I find I need to put some closure in place now that the board have agreed to the changes and it's going to be time to head back to New York. After reading that plan of yours it's obvious you know me. And you know that all the time I'm up at that house I'm going to be thinking about what's going to happen after, and I'm thinking that's the only way I'll get through it.'

'Let me just get this clear in my head. Tonight, after spending some time with your family, you're going to let me seduce you?'

'Well, you're certainly going to take me to dinner. I may or may not let you perform the trick with the chopsticks that you mention.'

'And after that?'

'Maybe I'll take a leaf out your book, and go with the flow.'

He almost caved under her silent scrutiny. There was a tiny furrow between her eyes that suggested she wasn't quite as in control of her emotions as she'd like him to believe. But then she surprised him for the third time.

'I'll need to take some personal time this afternoon.'

'What for?'

'To get everything ready. For tonight.'

Wait, what, she was really going to agree to this?

'Very well,' he found himself saying, 'You can have the entire afternoon.'

Chapter Seven

In the intimate confines of the limousine Amanda inhaled Jared's woody cologne and felt her nerves stretch tighter.

Were they really going to do this? Of course they were going to do this, hadn't she just spent the entire afternoon shopping for this? Or to clarify, the thing that would happen after the family pit-stop.

She was so wired, she could hardly function.

Staring out of the tinted black window she wondered how she'd even made it as far as getting into the car.

She had been so sure he was going to play fair with her. Behave like a gentleman. Let her off the hook. Brush her silly plan aside and show her how easy he was going to make it for her to do so, as well. She was Mikey's sister, for heaven's sake. He wasn't supposed to call her on the plan and tell her she had free reign to implement it.

And now, having shown faith in her ability, the very least he could do was help her out a little to get the ball rolling.

She chewed down delicately on her cherry lip gloss. It wasn't as though she hadn't used her feminine wiles on guys before. But, guys weren't Jared. Jared was somehow different. Jared was used to being in control. Jared didn't give up that control for anyone.

The fact that he was willing to relinquish that control for her—what did that mean, exactly? She kept needing to take the answer to the next level and make it mean more.

Her tongue snaked out to soothe her lip. Maybe knowing exactly what she had planned for him *was* his ultimate control?

'So where are you taking me to dinner?'

She jumped a little at the sound of his soft question.

'The Golden Palace. It's supposed to be the best Chinese restaurant in London.'

'Is that why you have chopsticks in your hair?'

'What? Oh,' her hand went to the loose knot at the back of her head, 'no, these are just for decoration.'

'Take them out.'

'I beg your pardon?' He didn't like them? The nerves doubled. In her plan, he didn't order her around. In her plan she was the one in control. In her plan he capitulated to their mutual pleasure.

'Take them out. They're too distracting. I can't focus on anything except... later. And I find I would like to be able to string a sentence together.'

Amanda smiled. His tight delivery melted away her nerves and reserve. 'A whole sentence huh? What happened to needing the distraction to get through the first part of the evening?'

'I'll make you a deal. You take those chopsticks out of your hair and I won't be looking at you like I want to devour you and then maybe *you'll* be able to string a sentence together!'

'Oh. I see. You're sort of helping me out. Well, that's very chivalrous of you.' She turned in her seat to make sure he had his full attention. Slowly she reached out with her right hand to pull the ornate chopsticks out of her hair. Shaking her head a little she allowed her curls to tumble down around her face and shoulders. 'That better?' she whispered, unable to hide the feline edge to her smile.

Jared groaned. 'Worse.'

Amanda released her seatbelt and slid over the leather seat.

'What are you doing?'

'Making it better.'

'Amanda—'

Whatever he was about to say was lost as she dragged the hem of her red Japanese silk dress up her thighs and smoothly shifted to sit astride him.

Jared went completely still. 'I don't seem to remember this being in your plan.'

'Maybe I'm improvising.' For balance she rested one hand against his beautiful white buttoned-up work shirt. She could feel the solid, hot pectoral muscle beneath; feel the heavy thump of his heart. Her own heartbeat tripled in tempo. 'Improvising isn't against the law, is it Jared?' Slowly, with her free hand she reached out to trace her forefinger against the fullness of his bottom lip.

In answer, Jared slid his hands up either side of her legs to grasp her hips and bring her into full contact with the hard ridge of his erection. Sucking the tip of her forefinger into his hot wet mouth, he proved he wasn't averse to a little improvisation himself.

Enthralled by the delicious sucking on her finger, Amanda bent her head to claim his lips and as he opened his mouth to let her in, the contact of her own finger against her tongue and then against his had her moaning into his mouth at the raw sensuality. He may have told her she kissed like an angel but he kissed liked the very devil. Withdrawing her finger she moved both hands up and into his hair. They clenched against his scalp as she changed the angle of her mouth; desperate to try and slake her thirst on his dark, sensual, drugging kisses.

She couldn't get enough of him.

She didn't know herself like this.

Hadn't known that she could want a man so badly, get so caught up, so quickly, that there was nothing but the thrill of falling thoroughly under his spell.

In fact she was so far under that it took her a moment to realise his hands were pulling hers gently out of his hair and putting them down on top of her thighs, trapping her into halting her movements and raising her head. Took her a moment, also, to realise he'd somehow shifted her to sit her further back on his strong, powerful thighs.

She frowned, not understanding and when his gaze shifted to the right and ahead she turned her head and instantly saw the outline of the driver. Chastened she turned back to look at him. He'd made her forget they were in the back of a moving chauffeur-driven limousine.

He was giving her a choice, a chance to put a stop to this, but the fact that she was still sitting on his lap, moving her hips with unconscious demand was signalling she didn't like that option. She was unable to force herself to move off him, no longer caring about the way he so easily made her discard all inhibition.

His hand left hers to press a button that had a blacked-out shield of glass rising discreetly between them and the driver.

Settling back in the seat he stared deeply into her eyes. Then, without his eyes leaving hers he moved his hands onto her dress, pushing the material up higher on her waist. Leaving her thighs and hips completely exposed.

He placed his hands lazily back on top of where he'd placed her own, at the top of her thighs. He breathed in and out, leisurely stroking his fingertips over her hands, forcing them to clench against her own thighs in response. When he stopped she couldn't prevent the tiniest moue of disappointment. He smiled wickedly and casually let his thumb move into the crease between hip and leg to stroke over the sensitive skin. Her hips bucked and she caught her lip to hold back a moan. She tried to move her hands out from under Jared's but he wouldn't release his grip. She was trapped astride his lap. Her hands held high up on her thighs, his thumbs free to stray to the sensitive folds between her legs. The sense of anticipation held her completely in the moment, completely in his thrall.

'This isn't in the plan,' she moaned again as his thumb brushed light circles over the damp silk covering her mound, whimpered when it drifted close, but not close enough to her clitoris.

'That plan is for later. This, right now, is for you.'

'Jared. No. You can't make me come on my own if I don't want to.'

'Now that sounds like a challenge.' He looked down at their hands and ran his fingertips into the splays between hers. Stroking up and down, testing whether she would keep them there if he moved his hands way. When her hands squeezed again against her open thighs and remained in position his smile turned pure carnal and damned if she didn't love it. His fingers moved to slowly stroke backward and forward over her and she could feel everything inside gathering to that one place.

'Jared. I mean it. I don't want to do this on my own.'

'But you're not on your own. I'm right here.'

'This isn't fair.' Her hips started to move faster as his touch became firmer. Her breathing grew laboured. 'This is about you being in control.'

'This is about me wanting to make you feel good. That's all. And I am making you feel good. Aren't I?'

Amanda's eyes rolled shut as her hips rolled forward.

'Are you going to let me finish this?' he asked quietly.

She couldn't believe she was going to let him bring her to climax like this. But then if he stopped she might just have to kill him and she really didn't see as she had any choice, what with her body moving intuitively to the rhythm he had set in motion. When his hands left hers again to move her thong to one side she kept her own hands where they were and let him.

Her eyes opened to watch him watching her; that ferociously focused expression on his face nearly enough to tip her over the edge. Dimly she was aware that she'd never chased the rush so diligently; never before wanted to prolong the ecstasy for so long. With his thumb repeatedly brushing against her clitoris she found herself moving on him with utter abandon as waves of pleasure rolled through every fibre of her being. But it was his fingers entering her with absolute precision that had her bucking out of rhythm as she contracted tightly around him, his expert caressing touch tipping her full-on into orgasm.

And it was the fact that she could hear his quiet encouragement that allowed her to give herself over completely to the experience of it. To ride out the storm until the very last shockwave pulsed through her, and when the trembling wouldn't cease she allowed him to gently adjust her position so that she was cradled against his chest. The solid, heavy, beat of his heart teasing her own into calmer rhythm, his hands soothing and stroking while she sat on his lap and basked in the sweetest sense of repletion.

As sanity returned, she realised she had effectively handed complete control over herself to a man who demonstrated such absolute authority that she couldn't help but feel a little in awe of him.

But when the car came to a stop minutes later and the driver advised that they had reached their destination she found her voice. 'There is no way I can walk in there.' Going from purring on his lap to the bright lights and noise of a large family house didn't feel appropriate.

She felt him reach over to the control panel. 'Drive around for fifteen minutes or so and then come back to the house.'

'Okay?' he asked her as the car pulled away once more.

She nodded and made to move away from him to try and pull herself together.

'I'm sorry. I couldn't just up and walk into that house and make small-talk. I must look—'

'You look incredible,' he interrupted.

'I *feel* incredible, although I guess right now that's not solely down to me.'

He puffed out his chest in an "if you want to say so" manner and just like that she was laughing—after one of the most intense experiences of her life. 'Okay, less with the modesty you, and more with the helping me find those chopsticks so I can fix my hair.'

He laughed himself and as they scouted around the back of

the limousine she cast him a quick look. He certainly looked less tense than when they'd gotten into the car earlier. That had to be a good thing, didn't it? He looked up at just that moment and smiled at her and she beamed back. He passed her the chopsticks and she smoothed her curls into its loose knot once more.

She heard the gravel crunch under the car's tires and automatically looked out of the window. She could see the lights of the large house in the distance. They had arrived. Again.

There was a fluttery, jittery feeling inside of her that she was finding difficult to describe until she realised with a start that what she was feeling was joyful. She tested the sensation but didn't like the clutch in her belly. Feeling joyful made her think of words like 'optimism'. And as such words like 'optimism' had been missing from her vocabulary for such a long time, panic flared. Reaching out a hand she grasped Jared's forearm.

'About that issue of control, I mean, I know you said it wasn't about you being in control; that it was about me. But you were in control—very much so. And I,' she didn't know how to ask for the reassurance she needed.

'Amanda, you must know what it does to a man to see that. I would never abuse that.'

She lowered her eyes. He didn't get it. 'I guess what I'm asking is could you be like that with me? *Would* you allow yourself to lose total and utter control like that?'

She saw his brief frown and the joy seeped out of her. She'd had to go and ask the difficult question. There was no need to panic after all, she thought, as she felt her emotions align themselves into their usual neat flat line, mellowing her and protecting her from reaching out for something that would only, in the end, wind up being taken from her.

'You're not talking about giving up control you're talking about losing it,' he surmised. 'Those are two very different things. Maybe you need to ask yourself why you would need someone to lose it like that.'

Not 'someone' idiot. You. She needed to know she could affect him as much and as deeply as he affected her.

The cold air from outside filtered in through the open car doors. She shivered and told herself it was better to get at the truth now rather than continue to fool herself.

'Were you ever going to allow me to seduce you tonight?' she asked, making herself look him dead in the eye. 'Did I get all dressed up for you for nothing?'

'Amanda, what you experienced just now, *how* you let yourself experience it... Was that down to you just as much as it was down to me? I don't know. Maybe it was equal. Maybe I'd like it better if it was equal. I guess what I'm saying is, we'll see, won't we?'

'I guess we will,' she paused, debating how honest to be with him and then, because he was her friend, knew she had to be. 'Jared, I want you to know—need you to know. I've never lost control like that before. I really need you to understand that. To understand what that means. And to accept what that means, even if you don't trust it.'

He tipped his head, running the permutations of her statement and she held her breath, willing him to give her something.

'It always amazes me how you can be so candid all the time.'

She busied herself getting out of the car so that he wouldn't see the disappointment but answered, 'Because, Jared, life is too short not to be.'

Jared followed slightly behind Amanda on the short walk up to the house. God, she'd come apart in his hands. Blissfully, wonderfully, completely, right in front of his eyes. The honesty of her response had shaken him to his core. Her need for reassurance after being so gut-wrenchingly honest with him had him quaking in his boots. She'd told him she trusted him. She'd proved she trusted him and still he couldn't give her what she needed. He'd just done to her what he would never let anyone do to him. He'd reduced her to absolute honesty, complete vulnerability, with no game-plan to fall back on. He felt ashamed of himself.

He'd have to make it up to her somehow. If he couldn't give himself totally over to her plan, he'd have to find some other way to make it up to her.

His mind was elsewhere, computing what had just happened, analysing its deeper meaning as they were shown into the drawing room.

A welcoming fire had been lit and hearing the crackle and spit he was instantly assailed by memories. Of a five-year-old Sephy goading him and Nora to spin around and around inside the long drapes covering the patio doors, nearly bringing the heavy brass rod down. Of being twelve and chasing the family cat Marmalade under the antique writing desk in the corner of the room and just managing to catch the family heirloom vase as it wobbled off the edge. Of being twenty-one and the night of Nora's birthday party and his father telling him how deeply disappointed in him he was. Of the sense of inevitability at finally hearing the words he'd been afraid of hearing all his life and the deep cut of shame that came with them. Of the brief light of freedom he knew he hadn't been able to conceal when his father had told him to get out.

That last memory was so strong that for a moment he didn't think he could move.

Amanda seemed to understand, because with a casual squeeze of her hand against his forearm she moved ahead of him to greet everyone and settle herself into a chair.

'Mum, Dad,' he greeted quietly from the doorway before nearly being knocked backwards when Daisy ran at him and locked her arms around his knees.

'Uncle Jared. You came, you came.'

Swamped by emotion, he looked down at his niece.

'Daisy,' Sephy said taking pity, 'you need to let Uncle Jared move, sweetie. In fact if you ask him nicely, I think he might just have a big surprise for you.'

'Really?'

'Really,' he nodded.

'Why don't you get someone to help you bring it in, Jared, maybe set it up in here?' Amanda asked, giving him the prompt he needed.

Daisy's eyes, when he and one of the staff brought the large doll's house into the room and set it away from the fire, were enormous. 'Is that really for me? Really?'

'Really,' he answered as she hopped with excitement. It seemed to be the only word he could get out past the lump in his throat. He looked around the room, careful to avoid his father's gaze.

'Where's Nora?' he asked.

'Oh, she's at a meeting, she'll be here soon,' his mother supplied.

'Meeting,' his father snorted, 'Euphemism for seeing that on-off man of hers, no doubt. Incredibly important day for KPC and where is the CEO? Out on a date, one suspects.'

'Oh Dad, leave her alone,' Sephy rebuked as she passed Amanda a cup of tea. 'Nora's entitled to celebrate however she sees fit. Apparently she was inspired by some report or file or something,' she said, winking outrageously at Jared and chuckling when Amanda choked on her drink.

Jared shot his sister a look that usually had businessmen cowering but his sister merely beamed back at him, unrepentant. He frowned. He'd forgotten how to do the sibling teasing thing.

His mother swiftly passed Amanda a napkin and settled back beside his father, who hadn't seemed to notice because he was saying, 'I expect your sister to know her responsibility first and foremost.'

Jared's hackles rose. Even now, with most of his family around him, and his time running out, his father only understood business. Was he supposed to fill in the blanks and report back on the day's events? It wasn't his place, damn it. Nora should have made the effort to be here. Surely she was aware their father would want to hear the blow by blow.

'Jared, why don't you give Daisy the grand tour,' Amanda instructed gently, coming to the rescue. 'Ask him lots of questions,

Daisy. He knows heaps about property. Jared, kneel down, so that you can see properly and Daisy doesn't feel like you're a giant.'

He did as he was bid and was busy taking the top off the house to expose the upstairs when he heard his father ask Amanda what her father did for a living. He paused with the large roof in his hands.

'My father was a lawyer and my mother was a teacher.'

Jared hadn't known that. So Mikey had followed in his father's footsteps. Was that deliberate? Mikey seemed passionate about law in his own right. But he must get a sense of peace from knowing his father would be pleased with his choice of career.

He tried looking objectively at his own father. Did Nora get the sense from him that he was proud of her? He hoped she did. She'd had to work hard enough to be seen by him. Jared hadn't been blind to the fact that at twenty-one he had been about to be handed KPC on a platter, leaving his sister floundering to find anything else that could compare, in her eyes.

'Was?' he heard his father ask and quickly felt the warning prickle for Amanda.

'That's enough. I didn't bring Amanda here to be interrogated.'

His father stared back at him with a look that said, 'Why did you bring her here?' He'd brought her here as a distraction and he suspected his father knew it. Suspected his father judged him for it and began to feel the first stirrings of anger at himself. Nothing about this place was supposed to leave its mark; he needed to remember that.

'It's alright, Jared, I don't mind talking about it,' with a brief look to make sure Daisy was playing contentedly with her house, she turned and said, 'It's just my brother Mikey and me, since our parents died in a hotel fire twelve years ago.'

'I see.' His father at least had the grace to look embarrassed. 'That must have been hard for the both of you.'

'Of course.' Her smile softened the words and Jared was reminded again of her candour. 'But you adapt. Heal. The ones who are gone are never forgotten. You learn to live again, albeit it differently.'

Jared watched, fascinated, as Amanda and his father exchanged a long look.

'Besides, Mikey was brilliant, making sure everything kept running. Of course it helps that he has this amazing, unswerving sense of responsibility, much like your own son.'

Jared's internal alarm went off but he didn't have a clue how to put a stop to her words.

'I'm sure you're aware how many staff your son employs, and how hard he works to provide them with a challenging yet stable working environment. Then there's the unwavering friendship he offers my brother and I. He's helped us through sometimes difficult times. And, of course, he came over here when Nora asked him.'

Jared didn't think she could have said anything more shocking if she'd tried. This wasn't so much bridging a gap as forging heavy foundations that he would rather have left for another lifetime altogether. But then, abruptly, he realised there was no other lifetime. There was only this one. This incredibly awkward one, which left him sitting dumbstruck, listening to Amanda using her candour to its sweetest effect, eliciting feelings within him that he didn't want to acknowledge, let alone come to need.

'Well,' his father turned assessing eyes on him, 'you certainly seem to have got better at choosing friends over the years.'

The anger was quick to spill forth. 'Oh Mikey and Amanda are more than friends, father. They're family to me.'

In the marked silence he immediately regretted his words. The flickering firelight danced over his father's pale and drawn face, forcing Jared to acknowledge how frail and beaten he looked. The anger seemed to emanate from him in waves, replaced with a horrible certainty that all his experience of planning, of analysing a situation and coming up with a solution, of being able to think on his feet, meant nothing.

Simple words proved elusive.

'Hi everyone, sorry to be so late,' Nora burst into the room, looking as if she'd just been on the best holiday of her life and Jared resented her putting him in the position of having to be here at all.

'Amanda and I were just leaving.'

'Not so soon,' his mother complained.

'We don't want to intrude on your celebrations,' he aimed at Nora.

'Don't be tiresome, Jared,' Nora said, 'the whole reason we have something to celebrate is because of you.'

He didn't think his father needed to hear that. Hell, turned out he didn't need to hear it either. Not as part of his closure. He was now very afraid he needed closure of a different kind; the kind that meant either he or his father reaching out farther than they knew themselves to be capable of.

He heard his mother's soft plea, 'Your father and I wanted to ask you about New York, hear all about your business; learn about your life.'

'You heard the boy,' his father dismissed, 'if he needs to get going...'

'No, Jeremy,' his mother said, louder and more desperate now. 'There may not be another time—'

'Nonsense, how long are you visiting for Jared?'

Visiting? It sounded so temporary. Made him feel all the more isolated from them all.

'We're leaving at the end of the week.'

'Oh but Jared,' his mother persisted, 'what about.., I mean, your father has a very important appointment tomorrow, perhaps you could stop by afterwards?'

'Now, now, Jared's done what he came here to do. Haven't you son? It's best he return to his own life.'

In his father's hollow stare Jared saw resignation, no, acceptance that the distance between them would remain unbridged. He couldn't look at him any longer. He thought he managed a nod in his direction but couldn't be sure. He needed to get out of the house. Right now. Dimly, he was aware of Amanda making their goodbyes on his behalf, vaguely he realised she was promising to drop in before flying back. He didn't care. Just wanted out.

Amanda let Jared brood in silence for a good few miles before she leant over to lightly touch him on the forearm.

He started slightly, looked at her sternly, and seemed to realise she was trying to get him to stay in the land of the living.

'What a bloody disaster,' he declared.

'Why do you say that?'

'Why do I...? I just insulted my sister in front of my father, ignored my other sister and caused tension in front of Daisy.'

'That's what families do, stupid. They push each other's buttons.'

'How the hell would you know?'

'What, you don't think Mikey and I push each other's buttons on purpose? Argue and shout the house down? It doesn't mean we don't love each other. You're just a little rusty on the whole family get-together scenario. You did way better than last time. Honestly. Last time, with your father, was real car-crash TV, I practically had to watch through my fingers. Lord knows what went down afterwards in that study of his. But this time you managed a sort of badly veiled insult-ridden conversation with him in front of the rest of the family and nobody passed out or anything. I wouldn't sweat it, you keep talking in those dark undertones of yours, responding to his careless statements that obviously hark back to whatever happened in the past, and the two of you are going to be back on solid ground in no time.'

Relief swept through her as he barked out a laugh but then she had to swallow the lump when in the next instant he looked lost.

'I'm sorry. I just—at the end—he looked so...'

She reached over and placed her hand on top of his. 'I know.'

'How are they going to cope if...when...'

'You'll all help each other. That's all.'

Chapter Eight

'Checkmate.'

Amanda looked down at the chessboard on the sofa between her and Jared, wondering how she'd so completely managed to leave herself wide open; defences down.

'You look like you're surprised,' Jared grinned. 'You didn't really expect to beat me at chess now did you?'

'And that's not at all sexist, or ageist or elitist or anything!' she threw back at him.

'Well, if you'd gone with my suggestion earlier, you would have had more incentive not to lose and you might have tried harder.'

'Jared King, only in some weird fantasy dream of yours was I ever going to go with playing strip-chess.' She tried to give him her haughtiest look, but somehow it didn't transfer when she was sitting on the huge mulberry-coloured suede sofa in her softest, most favourite grey tracksuit, her knees pulled up to her chest.

A night built for seduction, this was now, most definitely not.

She'd made the decision for the both of them in the back of that limousine when she'd realised Jared wouldn't be able to stop his mind doing its circular thing, analysing the evening until that computer in his head threw out a solution on how to get past needing closure, and had worked out instead how he could reach out to his father before it was too late.

As soon as she'd given the driver the instruction to return to the apartment Jared had leant his head back and closed his eyes to think. She'd held her tongue and held his hand.

Once in the apartment she'd poured him a double measure and excused herself to change out of the slinky dress, spikes and chopsticks ensemble. She wasn't altogether certain he'd even noticed. But by the time she'd joined him on the sofa, balancing two plates with omelettes on, he seemed a little more present.

'Where do you fancy going tomorrow?' he now asked.

'You were serious about going sightseeing?'

'Sure. Nora and I have a few more meetings lined up but tomorrow's completely free.'

'In that case I want to go up in the London Eye.'

'Great idea.'

'I want to do Buckingham Palace. The Tower of London, Houses of Parliament, Tate Britain and Tate Modern, The V and A—'

'Okay, we may not have time to do all that in one day.'

'—and Madame Tussauds, you know, your waxwork thingy.'

'Madame Tussauds? Are you actually serious?'

'Uh-huh, definitely going to need a bit of cheese-factor after all that culture.'

'Right. You know I really am sorry I haven't been a better host and shown you around a bit more.'

Amanda leaned her head back against the sofa and sighed contentedly. 'It's really okay. We came here to work, and now I've got all these new skills to take back with me.'

'I've always suspected you had serious skills. I may have wondered when you planned to use them...'

'I would have got around to it eventually.'

'Yeah? What about your whole "life is too short" ethos?'

'Okay. You got me.'

'It's okay to admit that you're alive, you know.'

She turned her head to study him. It was weird, she thought, as it turned out ever since she'd come to know him she'd started feeling as if she was awakening. She'd just been refusing to admit it to herself. For the longest time she'd only ever thought of him as a friend and she found it difficult to cultivate friends, found it hard to find people who 'got' her and were happy to let her be who she was. The close friends she did have were like family.

Jared had let her be who she was up to a point, and then he'd started looking and pushing her to grow. And now they were here, and she was looking at him not as a friend so much as...

Aware she was straying into dangerous territory, she shifted her head back, front and centre so that she could stare out of the window, out into the dark night with its hundreds of twinkling, illuminated apartments in the distance.

'So I've fallen in love with London,' she declared.

'So soon,' Jared teased, 'she hasn't even shown you her best qualities yet.'

'It's the sense of continuity; all the people who move through her streets, creating so much history.' She sat up a little straighter, warming to her subject, '—the towers that go up because there isn't space to build anywhere but up. The fact that old buildings sort of breathe in to make room for them.' She stretched out her legs, propping them on the coffee table. Pointing her toes she said, 'I love cities. Don't you? They're so alive with possibility.' Out of the corner of her eye she saw Jared looking at her polished red toenails. Pulling her knees back up to her chest she rushed on, 'It's like with KPC, all those years ago, starting out with just a couple of buildings and now there are hundreds of buildings, each with their own story.' She let herself look at him for one brief moment. 'That history was preserved today. Thanks to you, KPC get to continue.'

'And to think I was going to come in and shut it all down.'

Amanda grinned. 'Nah. Not you. Never you.'

'That was my plan.'

'That might have been your twenty-fifth plan,' she scoffed. 'But your first one was really to come over and assess the situation, take a look at the Kings and see what life had made of them in your absence.'

'Oh really? That was my plan was it?'

'Yep, your second one was to show them a little of what you'd made of yourself in the process.'

'If that was my plan all along, why did I need you with me?'

'To distract you from thinking about introducing plan twenty-five if you found them unwelcoming, or found yourself over-whelmed. That and the fact you knew you could introduce me to your family without me assuming something more significant.' She leaned over slightly to poke him in the arm for emphasis, 'And you knew I'd call the situation as I saw it.'

Jared's laugh was deep and throaty. 'You've had other people tell you you're outrageous, right?'

'Sure. Outrageous and right!' She turned her head just in time to catch his smile and then he frowned and stared down at his hands.

'So, how do you see it then?' he asked.

Quietly and carefully she said, 'I see that you could have come back before now. You would have been welcomed.' When the shutters fell into position she took a breath and carried on. 'But I think you'd never have allowed yourself to believe you really could come back because to do so would mean you'd have to forgive yourself for whatever it was that happened. And whatever it was has driven you and shaped you and made you become the success you are, so I guess, why would you? I mean, what if you forgave yourself and suddenly that drive, that reason, that *need* to push yourself, was gone?'

This time when she turned her head it was to find him staring back at her, his expression rueful.

'Hey, you asked,' she said. 'Anyway, it's just me saying it. You know me. You know you can trust me.'

'What else do you see?'

'Your family are a bit formal sometimes, but that's to be expected after so many years of structure bred into them all. Actually, I really like them. Nora comes across all proper and reserved but her passion for KPC runs deep and she had the guts to fly to you for help. Sephy lives her life on her terms, bringing up Daisy right in front of your father's eyes, showing him how impossible it is not to love someone so innocent. Your mother is the balancing force your father depends on and your father gave Nora a chance and then his support to rise to the very top of what is still a male-dominated business world.'

When he didn't comment, merely stared down at his hands, she continued, 'They're quite an impressive bunch. You slot in well with them. You do know how lucky you are, right? That it's not too late?'

She worried she'd said too much, but he had asked. And she knew he had to see his family history evolving right before his very eyes. The onus was on him if he wanted to become part of it.

'You must miss your parents,' he said, throwing her a little off balance.

'I try not to. Try not to miss the chapters of Gray family history that are lost forever. The little things like why they did the things they did, how they developed into the people they were. There's no one to ask about who they were as people, you know, rather than parents. And it's hard, sometimes, to work out if I do things because of them or because of what happened to them.' She shrugged her shoulders at the futility of it all. 'At a certain point, you have to let it go and just be who you are, be in the moment.'

'Be in the moment...'

'Uh-huh. You should try it once in a while. Might give that brain of yours a rest.'

In the next instant she found herself confiding, 'My parents would be embarrassed about where my life is at right now.'

'I'm sure they'd be extremely proud of both their children.'

'Mikey maybe. Me? Not so much. Can't really blame them.' She smoothed the soft material of her tracksuit over her knees. 'I'm sure when they made those plans that all parents make for their kids, you know, their hopes and dreams and projections for them, well, I'm fairly certain they wouldn't have come up with the sort of sitting around and waiting thing I've been doing for the last couple of years.'

'So, a little less living in the moment and a little more of a plan, is that what it needs to be about for you now?'

'Yep.' There. She'd said it. And it didn't really feel so scary.

'But for you, right, not for your parents and not for Mikey?'

'Right. For me.' She was pleased the conviction came so easily. Pleased she felt a plan for her future forming. Loose, nothing too tied down, but there nevertheless. She waited for the familiar stirring of panic, a little confused when it didn't beat down the door to emerge in a crazy whirl from the room she kept it in. 'You must be rubbing off on me Professor Plan!'

She got up off the sofa and stretched her arms up to the sky, yawning loudly. 'Of course it probably helps that you're insanely hot, too,' she said without thinking. When she looked down it was to catch Jared staring at the skin exposed at her midriff.

He rose from the sofa in one sinuous movement to stand in front of her. She found herself licking her lips and taking a step backwards because hadn't they both agreed, albeit it tacitly, that this was not the night for something to happen between them? As Jared continued to stand before her, staring down into her eyes with such intensity, Amanda worried she was going to have to remind him in some way about their agreement. Of course if she hadn't made the "insanely hot" crack.

He picked up her hand, turned her palm over, and slowly brought it to his lips to place a kiss at its centre. Her senses went crazy off the chart, eyes closing to savour the sensation, toes curling into the deep luscious pile of the carpet.

He stroked his thumb over the pulse point at her wrist and she knew he must be aware of the 'putty' effect he was having on her. 'Amanda. Thank you for tonight. For what you said to my father earlier this evening. For the things you said about my family.'

'It was all true, Jared.'

'All the same, thank you.'

'You're welcome.' She stood toe to toe with him. The longer he continued to stare down at her, the more she wavered. 'I guess it's getting late,' she made to tug her hand away. Was surprised, excited, when he didn't let go.

'I guess it is.'

'Jared—' she broke off. Didn't know how to let what was happening between them just happen. Wasn't sure she'd withstand the effect on her heart if she did let what was happening happen. They'd shared so much tonight already. She had that joyful feeling again but didn't know how to grasp onto it and hold it to her. Didn't know how to believe in it.

She couldn't trust that they could just have sex. She had a feeling he'd take her on a journey, an adventure of body, spirit and mind. That was the problem. She hadn't had occasion to share spirit and mind. She'd venture that he hadn't either. Maybe they'd figure it out together, except, maybe the first time with him it would easier if it was just sex. Less to lose. Less to make a fumble of.

She felt him reach out to tuck her hair gently behind her ear. Felt his fingers sweep over her hairline at the base of her neck to gently massage the knots. Something of her indecision must have shown on her face because she heard him sigh and then say, 'sleep well, Amanda,' before withdrawing his hand and turning to walk away.

Her hand went up to touch the back of her neck, where his fingers had been.

Okay, had she just turned down Jared King—the man she wanted with every fibre of her being—just because she'd been silly and wavered for an instant while he looked at her full of gorgeous intent? Well wasn't she the biggest fool ever to walk the face of the planet?

Confused, her body tight and now fully prepared to pout its way through the night; she turned and walked over to the large window to stare unseeingly out of it.

She tried telling herself it was for the best, that they were destined to remain friends and that that wasn't really such a bad thing. She tried to tell herself that she'd be able to go sightseeing with him the next day and actually appreciate the views before her and not think about how she wanted his hands all over her. She tried telling herself he needed more time to process what had happened with his family, as if his mind wasn't razor-sharp, as if he wouldn't already have come up with a plan of action.

She looked out at the apartments across the river. She couldn't totally see into them, but she had it in mind that everyone else within them was busy living their lives. Really living them. Unafraid.

She bowed her head to rest it upon the glass. She wanted to be like them. She wanted to walk down the corridor to his room and boldly slip inside. But she needed to know she could deal with the after.

This time she was going to think before she acted.

'You know I've been thinking about that "insanely hot" remark you made.'

Amanda's head shot up at the sound of his voice. Her eyes met his in the reflection in the window. Her heart started thumping, 'Well, you do like to think,' she mused.

He started unbuttoning his shirt as he made his way over to her and all thought process went right out the window. She wasn't even aware her own hands had gone to the zip of her tracksuit top. But when she saw his eyes track the movement, saw him swallow, she knew and started lowering the zip.

As she dragged the zipper down the last inch of material he arrived behind her. She closed her eyes and breathed in deeply, wanting to feel the heat of him at her back. With her eyes closed she heard him drag his shirt tails from his trousers. When she would have turned to take in what was sure to be the incredible view of Jared King in one of his starched white work shirts unbuttoned, he took a step to close the distance and brought his hands to where hers rested on the zipper at the base of her tracksuit top.

'It occurred to me,' he dipped his head to whisper in her ear, 'I ought to thank you for the "insanely hot" remark.'

'Compliment where it's due and all that,' she managed before her eyes crossed in pleasure as he sucked her earlobe into his mouth.

'It got me thinking about what you said about living in the moment.'

'It did?'

'Mmmn. Ask me what I want right now.'

She couldn't.

'Ask me,' he repeated.

'Okay.' With heart in her hands, she tipped her head back against his chest and asked, 'What do you want, Jared?'

'You,' he nuzzled her hair out of the way to gain access to her neck, 'I want to be with you.' His lips moved to settle against her pulse point. His tongue snaked out to lick and her eyes rolled back into her head. 'Just you and me. No family getting in the way. No business getting in the way.' His hands squeezed against hers in conspiracy. 'No worry about "after" getting in the way.' His hands moved with hers to disengage the zip from its fastening. 'Just you and me. In this moment. What do you think?'

'Oh, you want me to think?' She felt him smile against her throat, but his hands remained with hers on either side of the material of her top. Waiting. Weighing up which way she was going to go. 'So now you're all about the living-in-the-moment thing, even though you're waiting for me to answer you, which is incredibly sweet.' She felt him move against her and smiled. 'Okay not sweet so much as incredibly hot.' She sighed, 'But I'm supposed to be all about working-to-a-plan now—'

'—but you already have a plan. You even gave it a title and bullet points. In it you clearly sited the healing properties of assuaging curiosity, sating needs and being able to deal with the after...after. Did you mean it?'

God, hearing her own words said back to her in her ear, like that. It all sounded so easy, so straightforward. 'I guess if we both know what we're getting into, that this can only ever be a one-off. Just to, you know, get it out of our systems. But this old tracksuit certainly didn't feature in any plan I wrote, in fact none of this is exactly according to how I set out—'

'So I'm improvising. Improvising isn't against the law, is it?'

She laughed, 'Oh, you're good.' Deep down inside she felt that joyful feeling again.

'Let me show you good.'

The joyful feeling took hold. 'Okay,' she said simply. 'I'm in your hands.'

His triumphant chuckle had goosebumps breaking out all over her skin, but it was his hands squeezing against hers that let her know he wasn't about to approach this too lightly. It was good to know because with Jared King, it would appear impossible for spirit and mind not to want get in on the act too.

And then she didn't have time to wonder if his spirit and mind were going to join the party because his large beautiful hands were parting the sides of her top and skating up her ribs to claim her breasts.

Her hands dropped to her sides to give him more access. They clutched against the edges of his own shirt material when he palmed her breasts and rolled her nipples between thumb and forefinger. She moaned aloud at the sensation, already caught up in The World of Jared and Amanda, where only the two of them existed.

She felt bereft when his hands moved to stroke over her collar bone and then he was dragging the material of her top down her shoulders.

'So beautiful,' he murmured.

She opened her eyes to see him staring at what he'd unveiled, the plate glass window acting like a mirror. Her heavy eyes moved to look at what he was so entranced by and she thought she did look beautiful, standing before the window with all the lights on, for anyone to see, with Jared's hands on her. She didn't care that the black night held potential voyeurs. She only cared that Jared was looking at her with such deep focus it took her breath away.

Her hands moved behind her to his belt buckle and Jared took a step away to facilitate her, helping her when she fumbled. She pulled the belt through its loops and dropped it on the floor. Her top joined it a second later.

Finally he let her twist in his arms to face him. Her eyes drank in his magnificent torso and desperate to touch what she was seeing she lifted her hand to let her fingers slowly investigate the expanse of muscled territory. As her fingers undulated over his abdominal muscles he breathed in sharply.

'You have no idea how much I've wondered what it would feel like having your fingertips drag their curious way over my body.'

'Yeah?' she sucked in her bottom lip in delight. 'What does it feel like?'

'Insanely hot' he groaned, closing his eyes and tipping his head back slightly.

She looked at him from under her lashes, the corded muscles in his neck standing proud, his eyes closed to savour her touch and suddenly she felt empowered; emboldened. She wanted to see just how much he was laying himself open to, just how gentle a touch he could register. She reached up on tiptoes, leant in and blew the gentlest breath against the beautifully corded muscle of his neck. He trembled and brought his head forward until his forehead rested against hers. He breathed out unsteadily, his hands flexing against her waist in response and she felt giddy that he would allow himself to feel so much with her. Suddenly, being with him wasn't about who was in control, or who was losing control, it was only about exploring, *revelling* in the connection between the two of them.

She stepped into the heat of his embrace, needing to get as close as possible, wanting to feel flesh against flesh. They both sighed at the contact, both inhaled, expanding their chests to press even closer.

She shivered as Jared's beautifully capable hands smoothed their way from her waist up her ribcage, skirting the undersides of her breasts and moving along the length of her arms to place them over his shoulders. When he was satisfied her hands were going to continue to cling in position around his neck he started swaying, dancing, moving his own hands to cradle her head and splay in the small of her back so that he could squeeze her impossibly closer to him still. She moved with him in a silent rhythm all of their own making, luxuriating in the feel of torso against torso, her hands moving into his hair and tugging his head down to claim his lips.

At the first touch of his tongue her mouth opened, fusing itself to his, drinking him in and beckoning him into her soul. Her breathing grew short and laboured as time and time again their lips moved over each other, under each other, their tongues brushing, stroking, entangling. Each kiss taking, each kiss giving back, until she was weak at the knees; dizzy with need. When her knees did buckle she felt Jared's grip on her tighten, felt him pick her up with ease and without his lips leaving hers, found herself being lowered. She gasped as her back hit the cold polished surface of the large dining-room table.

'Too clichéd?' he said, grinning down at her.

She shook her head and stretched herself out sinuously against the smooth surface, 'Wildly practical.' She leaned up on her elbows and smiled. 'You seem to still have clothes on.' She looked up into his emerald-green eyes. 'Take them off for me, Jared.'

That sexy side-smile of his emerged. She watched him slowly shrug out of his shirt and her mouth went dry. Watched greedily when his hands went to the fastening of his trousers. When he paused, her eyes flew to his, rejoiced in watching him watching her—rejoiced in that beautiful granite jaw clamped tight with need, his beautiful skin flushed and stretched tight. Then, unable to help herself her eyes moved again to his trousers, wanting to watch him undress for her, needing to see the rest of his spectacular body. She saw his hand reach into his trouser pocket, her eyes widening when his hand withdrew a full handful of condoms to trickle them over the table surface. 'Er, will we be using all of these, then?'

'Thought we might.' He grinned that special carnal grin of his and stepped out of his trousers.

Looking at him she was pretty sure her own grin turned carnal, 'I'm loving that thinking thing you do,' she said as she let him scoot her closer to the edge of the table, felt his palms at her hips and then felt them move over her skin as he tugged her tracksuit bottoms and underwear down her legs and tossed them casually over his shoulder, 'loving the action better,' she said, as he moved to take a foil packet and sheath himself before lowering that sexy mouth of his to take her breast into his mouth.

His hot tongue swirled lazily around her nipple and the breath hissed out of her. Her legs clamped compulsively around his hips to hold him close. Her hands flattened against the table. And as his hands smoothed up her thighs, making her tremble in anticipation, she moved against the length of him and was transported into a world of sighs, moans and groans as his mouth left her breasts to trail kisses down the centre of her torso. She began to tremble in earnest, her body moving, responding to his every touch, craving him completely and she wondered if there wasn't any song he couldn't get her body to sing.

Fuelled by her trembling Jared's kisses burned hotter, harder, his mouth hungry now as it roamed over her, feasting off her; his whole being concentrating on soothing and exciting her. Enthralling and enticing her. Building her higher and higher until she was consumed with the need to feel connected to every part of him.

Desperate now to feel him moving inside of her, she dug her heels into the edge of the table and scooted upwards to lie fully upon it. Hungry for his touch she was pleased when he clambered panther-like onto the shiny surface with her. As he settled his weight over her she was utterly transfixed by the intensity in his expression. Unexpectedly moved by the way he gently brushed back the hair from her forehead.

And gasped when in the next instant he plunged into her, her body rising up to meet his even as the 'Oh, but,' escaped from her mouth. She had so wanted to touch him as he'd touched her. Spend time drawing sensation out of sensation, wring every last drop of pleasure out of their bodies before they built the journey together again.

As if able to read her mind Jared smiled and whispered, 'Next time,' into her mouth.

And then he began to move in earnest. And she loved the way he moved on her, in her, over her. Loved how he drove everything in the world from her, but him, in this moment, with her. Loved the way he loved her. Loved...

She turned her head and watched their reflection in the window and thought they looked magnificent together. Jared's supple muscles stretching and pulsing, making her moan at the thrill and power of it all. Making her need this in her life; making her need him in her life. Changing her forever with his expert touch. Like this was what she was made for. Like she was made for him.

Jared turned his head to see what she was looking at. Moved harder within her when he realised she was looking at the two of them together.

'Just you and me,' he whispered, moving more urgently now, claiming all her attention.

'Just you and me,' she answered, looking up at him, grasping him to her and convulsing around him.

Chapter Nine

'What the...' Jared winced and opened one eye as he felt the sharp flick against his butt. He was just in time to see Amanda's hand returning lightning quick to her mouth to try and smother her giggle.

He was laying on his stomach, on, thank God, the huge soft bed in Amanda's room.

'Well, it's your own fault,' she said by way of an apology, 'you weren't supposed to be so good I can't get enough! And we do have one condom left.'

Had they really gotten through all but one of the condoms? He frowned. After the table, he remembered the sofa—twice and then, much later, the floor, before he'd declared their next time was definitely going to be in bed, so they'd made it into Amanda's room; just.

Now, she was watching him quietly, and he wondered how long she'd been lying there next to him, working out how to keep things light. Keep things simple.

It wasn't going to be easy. He hadn't expected her to be so invigorating to his ego; so captivatingly responsive in his arms. And he sure as hell hadn't expected her to fit him so beautifully; like she was made for him.

He only had to look at her and he was reliving the breathy catch in her voice just before she came, her sweet muscles clamping around him, making him feel invincible. But concentrating on those two things was never going to help him keep it light and simple and the doubt pushed and pushed and he closed his eyes as the wave of guilt crashed over him until a tiny sound had his eyes opening again.

'Hey,' his heart jolted inside his chest as he saw the tears gathering. Quickly, he turned to gather her into his arms.

'Sorry. Kind of wrung out, physically and emotion—'

He kissed her before she could finish the sentence. Soothed his hands down her arms and tucked her more tightly against him.

'Jared?'

'Yes?'

'What happens now?'

Now they continued living in the moment. Anything else was inconceivable. 'Maybe I don't let you out of this bed until it's time to pack.'

'Teeny bit impractical?'

'Is this scaring you?' he reared up to look at her. 'Am I scaring you?' He really hoped not. He was… he searched for the word. Happy. Amongst all the madness that was working out how to be a member of the King family again, she made him happy.

'I woke up and, well, I guess I'm more used to you being the man with the plan. Thought I'd better find out if there was one. I mean I know I had the original plan, but well, I just wanted to see if we were on the same page.'

Stroking her incredibly soft skin he focused on the word happy. Ought to be simple enough, he thought. 'What would you say if I told you I'd had the best night of my life and that I'd like us to continue while we're in London? Push the old: what happens in London stays in London, to the max?'

He felt her tense in his arms and forced himself to let her answer in her own time, however she wanted to answer.

'I'd say, ditto.'

'Well, then,' his heart sort of sang, surprising him. 'That's settled.'

'Okay. Good. Settled,' she sighed against his skin as he rolled her into the middle of the bed and starting nuzzling her neck.

He smiled as he felt the quickening in her breathing, muscles that were a moment ago languid, now pulling taut with need. Need for him.

God, she tasted better that anything he'd ever tasted in his life. How was that possible? He couldn't let her go, not yet. Not until they were done with each other. It wouldn't be fair. It wouldn't be right. Soon, he would work it all out but right now? Right now he needed to feel her go up in flames. Needed what that gave him.

He shuddered as he drove into her, groaned when she rose to match his thrusts. Looked into her eyes and felt the rest of the world magically disappear.

Amanda awoke feeling fantastically sated. Turning over in bed she stretched dreamily, squinting against the watery sunlight filling the room. When her stretch didn't encounter the heat of Jared's body she frowned and dragged herself into a sitting position.

Slowly opening her eyes, she listened for him but the apartment sounded empty. She was tempted to lie back down on the beautiful silk sheets and just wait. Waiting for Jared to come back and make her body sing for him again didn't seem wrong. In fact it sounded like a plan.

Settling back down amongst the covers she spied the folded piece of paper with her name on propped up against the bedside table and scrambled up again to snap it up.

'Getting supplies ;-) Maybe taking my father to his hospital appointment. Back after lunch to take you out. J'

Oh.

Suddenly spending a few hours waiting made her feel a little too needy. Not good, she silently chastened herself, looking around her at the rumpled linen, wondering what she should do with her morning. Getting up would be a good start, she supposed;

imbibing copious amounts of coffee, even better.

She stood up, wrapped the top sheet around her and padded out to the living area in search of coffee. Her eyes lighted on the neatly stacked pile of clothing on the sofa. Jared must have put them there. She wondered what had been going through his mind as he'd picked up each piece from where they'd been discarded around the room, evidence of how they hadn't been able to get at each other fast enough.

She switched the coffee maker on, reached for a mug; stared into the distance. Left on her own, her mind started grinding its gears. Preparing her for processing exactly how she could have fooled herself so completely into believing they could enjoy a quick tumble and that would be that. She'd used every cliché in the book to justify indulging her curiosity for him. The fact that he'd surpassed even her wildest dreams didn't sate that curiosity it only reinforced a deeper need.

Too scary, she breathed; pouring strong coffee into a mug and walking back to her room to pace.

She needed to do something to take her mind off thinking about Jared and how he had in the space of one night forced her to think about the structure she had drawn, the boundaries she had set and the plan that should have had her believing everything would be okay when the sex ended and the friendship re-began. When the sex ended... It had barely begun, and already she was panicking about it ending. But it would end. Everything did, didn't it, and usually when she was just getting used to having it.

She felt the panic and reminded herself she had chosen this. The trick was not to want it too much. Not to wind up needing it too much. All she had to do was go determinedly where she was so used to going—along with the flow. Enjoy the moment. Respect it for what it was. Appreciate it for what it was.

Her heart started to ache. She needed a distraction. Reaching for her laptop she settled herself in the middle of the bed and began researching wedding photography.

She lost track of time. Would never be able to pinpoint the exact moment her search changed to research for setting up her own wedding photography business. Only knew that the loose plan she'd had forming in her head for days felt right, solid, good.

Felt like a lifeline.

Hours later she set the laptop aside so she could search the apartment for pen and paper. Naked, she ran into the living area, needing something to sketch out the logo that had just popped into her head.

Jared's body sprung to attention as the lift doors opened to showcase Amanda's beautiful, naked form.

Caught in the middle of the room, she looked at him, blew a strand of hair out of her face and shyly said, 'Hi.'

It was the sweet shyness that had him wading into the room, hauling her into his arms and kissing her senseless. He'd only been gone a few hours. Didn't want to admit to himself that he'd missed her.

'Hi,' he echoed sometime later when he reluctantly relinquished her lips to breathe.

'I got your note,' she said, smiling up at him. 'Did you take your father to the hospital?'

'Yeah. We, well, we sorted some stuff out.'

'That's fantastic. He listened to you fairly?'

'I think I kind of caught him unawares. It was a difficult appointment and afterwards he was very,' he ran a hand through his hair, trying to grasp the right words, 'Let's say he was a lot fairer than I deserve.'

'Jared, he's your father. Even if you never tell me what happened all those years ago I can tell you that fathers are supposed to forgive their sons. Fathers are supposed to lead by example, step up to the plate and teach their children.'

Sometimes Jared thought Amanda's expectations of people were too high. Maybe that was because she had lost her parents at such a young age. Maybe that was because she looked at familial relationships through rose-tinted glasses. But when she spoke with such simple conviction it sure made a person want to behave better and to try and exceed those expectations of hers.

'So, what have you been up to while I've been out?' he asked. Determined to start rising to those expectations by ignoring his more base instincts. A hard task when she was naked and in his arms.

'Oh.' She licked her lips and he closed his eyes against the need pulsing through him. 'Well, I've been working on a few ideas. I just came out here for some paper actually.' She wriggled out of his arms and bent to rummage in her bag at her feet. 'Voila,' she exclaimed pulling out a pad of paper and a pen. Quickly she wrote something down, drew a few lines and hugging it to her turned to go back into the bedroom.

He followed the sway of her hips as if in a trance.

'You know I said it was all about the plan for me now?'

His heart missed a beat. Every selfish bit of him wanted to persuade her to forget about any plans and focus on living in the moment. If he could do that for her, why couldn't she do that for him?

'I've been having this idea—well actually it's more of a plan, which is pretty big for me. I mean I'm going to have to work hard, really hard, maybe even go back and do some more training,' she tipped her head to the side, 'but I'm really excited.'

Go away and train? Work really long hours? Jared felt something shift within him, 'Amanda, what's the plan, sweetheart?'

'Oh.' She pulled in a deep breath. Looked nervously at him and rushed out, 'I'm going to start my own wedding photography business!'

He wondered if she even knew she'd said *I'm going to* and not *I want to*. He was happy for her. Proud she'd finally found which dream to work towards. And yet... 'New businesses usually have high start-up costs,' he frowned. He could see the determination on her face. Soon he was sure she'd soar with those plans of hers—

'I know that, Jared.'

—and possibly fly far, far away from him. He didn't like the feeling. 'It's hard to make a profit the first couple of years.'

'I know that too,' she said carefully.

'I'm just saying,'

'What? What are you saying? How will I afford to move out?'

'Well, I thought that was the plan. To get a job that afforded you a place of your own.'

'So this is a new plan. A different plan. A plan, Jared, that includes budgets and forecasts and steps that I need to take in order to move out.'

'Well, that's great then.' He was *not* going to rain on her parade. He was going to give her the encouragement she always gave him. 'Get dressed and I'll take you out to celebrate.'

She watched him for a moment, in that quiet way of hers before shrugging her shoulders and heading off to the bathroom.

He heard the shower turn on and his eyes were drawn to the laptop. He moved over to the bed, bent to skim through her research. It was impressive; had him scrolling back to the beginning to look at her business plan. Had him thinking again about start-up costs and how she deserved a break.

***

From the dance floor Amanda looked over to where Jared was seated, deep in conversation with his sisters.

After their strange and stilted conversation about her work plans they'd shared the most perfect afternoon, hiding from the rain, wandering in and out of museums, lingering in bookshops.

The beat slowed a notch, became heavy and she let it pulse through her. She saw Jared turn to look at her.

She moved her body for him as she watched him watching her—his gaze unabashedly predatory, signalling to every male on

124

the dance floor that she was taken.

And she knew that she was.

Thoroughly. Completely.

Temporarily, she made herself say.

This, whatever it was between them, was *not* a prelude to adopting the name Latest Limpet. She knew the score. After all, she had written the rules for it.

Suddenly tired she slipped through the crowd on the dance floor and wandered around the "World Stage" room of Madame Tussauds.

Picking up a fruity cocktail from an A-list lookalike waiter she found her eyes inexorably driven to the fine cut of Brad Pitt's dinner jacket. Interesting. She was pretty sure she'd read that full body-casts were taken of the celebrities. Angelina Jolie stood close by giving her a look that seemed to say "go ahead, if you dare".

Some dares, dares that were frivolous and harmless and helped drive out all thought of a certain broodingly handsome man sitting at a table watching her, were impossible to ignore. Her hand reached out. In a room full of waxwork dummies and party goers who would know?

'I'm pretty sure touching isn't allowed.'

Amanda jumped and turned around to face Jared. 'And how do you know that's what I was going to do?' she asked, trying and failing miserably not to look like she'd been caught with her hand in the cookie jar.

He raised an eyebrow and grinned. 'Are you enjoying yourself?'

'I really am. It was great of Nora to set this up for the KPC staff. I didn't know they held parties here after hours.'

'Enough of the cheese factor for you?'

She smiled. To be able to throw on a sparkly cocktail dress and come here to have a boogie amongst the waxwork celebrities. It was perfect. Fun. Light. Uncomplicated.

She ran her eyes over Jared in his fitted black shirt and trousers.

Lord, he was sexy. Hot. Totally complicated.

Without realising her eyes turned back briefly to Brad Pitt.

'Would you like me to turn my back so that you can cop a quick feel?' Jared said dryly before turning around.

This time when Amanda looked at Angelina Jolie, her eyes seemed to be saying 'what are you looking at mine for when you've got a perfectly fine real one to check out'.

Without stopping to think through her actions, she tipped Angelina the wink and passed her hand slowly over Jared's butt.

'I cannot believe you just did that!' he said, whipping back to face her.

'You're kidding right? You practically ordered me to.'

'So outrageous.' He shook his head slightly and smiled, 'You want to get out of here?'

'What about your sisters?'

'Right now all I can think about is you and the way you danced for me and,' he moved in closer, bent his head to whisper, 'number fourteen on your "how" list.'

'Ah. Number fourteen,' her breath caught and she smiled. 'Possibly I've never mentioned I studied gymnastics for a while.'

'Right, we're getting out of here. Now.'

Sexy. Hot. Totally complicated. She ignored the last part, tipped back the rest of her drink and placed her hand in his.

They didn't speak in the taxi on the way home. Nor in the lift that zoomed them up to the apartment. When the lift doors opened Amanda walked towards the glossy white breakfast bar unit to put down her purse, Jared waited the second for it to hit the surface before grabbing her by the hips, turning her around and walking her backwards to the nearest available wall. He pushed her against the hard surface, leaned in, placed his hands on either side of her head, caged her in and ordered, 'Kiss me.'

She nodded once, before reaching up to seal her luscious mouth over his. Electricity shot through him.

And the maddening swirling vortex of need that had been gathering inside of him for hours grew stronger, threatening to beat out of control. 'Again,' he ordered when he felt her lips slide off his to drag in much-needed air.

Again she kissed him, her hands moulding the shape of his back. But it wasn't enough. He needed to feel her hands all over him. Shaping, clenching, clutching; demanding. Like his was going to do to her, he needed to know that the clawing hunger would come to claim them both. His hands came off the wall to start unbuttoning his shirt and she seemed to understand because in the next instant she was ripping at it. He groaned as her hands found flesh, shuddered when her nails scraped lightly down his pecs. His hands slid under the hem of her dress, dragging it up and off her body. Next, he peeled off her bra and thong until she was naked and her honey-golden skin beckoned for him to gorge on. And he intended to gorge. Needed to take his fill before this thing he had for her got away from him completely.

She let him spin her around so that he could slide his lips over the slope of her shoulders, along her spine, across her buttocks and down her legs. Let him brand every inch of velvet skin with his lips until she was begging him to turn her around and start again, which he did, the pleasure mounting until it was thrumming through every fibre of his being.

The sounds she was making drove the need deeper and frantic suddenly, he reached into his pocket and tore open a condom and then her hands were there, taking it from him, unzipping his trousers to free him and put it on. With ease, he lifted her legs to wrap them around his hips and as he readied himself at her entrance he looked into her eyes and she said not one word. Just smiled at him like he could do anything in the world he wanted to her. His head spun; the fact that she trusted him so. She was too generous with her spirit. And he was too damn selfish because he wanted everything she could give him and more. Wanted it like he'd never wanted anything and the strength of feeling had him fighting the pervading panic and the only solution was surely to plunge into her all the way up to the hilt; needing desperately to feel her surrounding him, his beautiful Amanda.

When her whispered pleas for more grew stronger, he gave her more, moving harder, faster, deeper. Until he was on fire, and his body was slick with sweat, and his heart was so full he thought it might burst. And when she told him she loved the feel of his mouth on her, loved the way his hands branded her, loved the way he moved within her he lost it completely; driving into her over and over again, her name a chant on his lips, until suddenly he was throwing back his head and emptying himself into her.

Sanity was slow to return but when it did Jared was certain of one cold fact.

He'd lost control.

Somehow, sweet, beautiful, outrageous Amanda had invaded the fortress he'd put up in his mind and unleashed the thought-less part of him he'd worked years to lock down. He dragged in a breath and raised his head to look at her.

She was still quivering against him. Her eyes were closed. A soft smile was on her face as her hands slid off his slick shoulders so that she could push her hair back off her face. She opened her eyes to look at him and wreaked havoc on his conscience. He swallowed back the guilt but it overpowered him in heavy, dark waves. He should have treated her with more care. Instead, he'd let his emotions take over, let the tiger out of the cage, bruised her, he now noticed as he looked at his fingerprints against her arms.

'Amanda, I—' he didn't know how to begin. How did he apolo-gise for having the best sex of his life, without reducing it to just that: sex. And it was so much more. She made it so much more. Hell, she was the first woman ever to make him feel as though blind need had taken over every corner of his mind and soul. To admit that would complicate everything, and yet she still deserved his apology.

The fact that she took pity on him, placing a gentle fingertip against his lips made him feel even worse. Bending to pick her up, he cradled her against his chest like a fragile flower as he carried her into the room he'd been using.

Very carefully he laid her down in the centre of the large bed, drew the covers gently up over her, before walking around to the side to slip in beside her.

The time making her comfortable hadn't brought any easy words to mind but he had to try.

'Don't you dare do it, Jared King,' she said, looking up at him. 'Don't you dare start apologising for something I actively encouraged.'

'I have to; I should have treated you with more finesse, with more—'

'Take a good look at me, Jared. Do I look in anyway hurt, frightened, overwhelmed?'

He looked down at her and all he could register was how damn beautiful she was. How right she felt lying next to him.

'Exactly!' she said, when he didn't answer. 'Besides, it's really me who ought to be apologising. I was really, *really* vocal!'

She looked alternately surprised and pleased with herself and from nowhere a rumble of laughter escaped him, soothing his soul and helping to banish the fear of hurting her. 'We're pretty good together, huh?'

'Are you kidding? Best I've ever had!' Her eyes popped and her jaw opened. 'Okay, that didn't come out right.'

'Oh no, that came out exactly right. I like your answer just fine. And if that's what losing control feels like with you, then I say, bring it. You bring the vocals.'

He linked his fingers with hers a thought suddenly occurring to him. 'Is that what you've been doing? Living your life quietly in the hope it will run smoothly?'

She turned in towards him. 'Maybe,' she whispered. 'Yes. I know it's been wrong.' Propping herself up on her elbow she looked down at him; tightened her fingers against his. 'What happened when you tried to take on the Fates? When you tried to step outside the plan they had for you?'

He thought back ten years. The tidal wave of shame coming so closely on the heels of losing control made him want to shut down. He didn't want to sully the image she had of him.

'Jared? What happened?'

But she deserved honesty. He paused and then quietly said, 'People got hurt.'

'Your family?'

He winced. 'Not just my family. Innocent people. Strangers.'

'That's a heavy weight to carry.'

But carry it he must, to help keep him from repeating his mistakes, from acting without thinking. He closed his eyes because he hadn't perfected his control, had he? In fact the second time he'd stepped outside a careful plan his best friend had lost the use of his legs. Guilt tore at him, making him move restlessly until Amanda's fingers stroked soothingly across his hand.

Logically, in his head, he understood that he wasn't really to blame for Mikey's accident. In his head he knew absolutely that Mikey didn't need him carrying any guilt because Mikey was truly happy and living a full life. But in his heart..? In his heart he was twenty-one years old again and his inability to follow a plan, his spontaneity, had caused someone pain.

'Being a King is quite the responsibility,' he said when he felt able.

'But, then, I imagine you were quite the responsible King.'

'I guess. Until I started questioning the career path mapped out for me at birth. Until I started to fear I'd never leave my own mark. That working at KPC would turn me into my father's puppet.' He smiled into the darkness, remembering the arrogance of youth. 'I wanted to be my own man. Forge my own destiny.'

'But that wasn't possible at KPC?'

He sighed. 'I tried. My father and the generations of Kings before deserved that. But I felt stifled; hampered by this creeping sense of inevitability that I'd fail because I simply didn't want it enough.'

'Surely your father understood? He'd had to accept the same

responsibility before you.'

'My father was younger than twenty-one when his father died and he took over at KPC. He didn't get a shot at looking at his options, didn't even realise he had any. I learnt today that even had he had the choice, he still would have chosen KPC.'

Jared thought back to the conversation he and his father had tried to have that morning and felt the same sense of frustration. 'I think he'll always feel I deliberately orchestrated events, deliberately burnt my bridges to force him into the position of firing his own son from the family business.'

'What did he fire you for?'

'Criminal damage to KPC property.'

When Amanda merely continued stroking her thumb over his hand, he turned his head to look at her. 'Not even shocked?'

'Not even. Jared, I know you. You wouldn't have, couldn't have...'

'What if I told you that during the May Day riots that year I was part of an anti-capitalist group who smashed in the windows and set fire to several KPC buildings? That several workers in the buildings suffered smoke inhalation and others received cuts from the glass flying in at them and that one worker suffered a heart attack whilst being evacuated.'

'I'd say that's tragic, but that it's baloney to say you were involved with something like that.'

Jared frowned up at her, his heart hammering loudly in his chest. 'You seem so sure. I was very angry that year; determined to reject KPC before it rejected me.'

'And yet I suspect your rebellion went more along the lines of riding around on your motorbike trying to find yourself. Your father should have known that, Jared.'

If he hadn't spent so much damn time riding around on his motorbike thinking only of himself, he would have been wise to what was actually happening. He sighed, moved restlessly against the mattress. 'Oh he did know it, eventually, when the police came to tell him I was totally exonerated from their enquiries. When they explained I had realised the group of ex-university friends I'd met up with a time or two were actually responsible, and that I'd gone straight to the police with my suspicions.'

'So did he then want to reinstate you?'

'The damage had already been done. I was guilty by association, particularly as one member of the group was the son of my father's biggest competitor. In order to salvage his son's reputation he slung the mud first and my father was very afraid it would stick.'

'But how could your father believe anyone over you?'

'Because the tension between us that year was already too high. Because his son had become a stranger to him, acting selfishly, defying the King plan. Because the responsibility of separating me from the potential fall of KPC fell solely to him. Protecting the business he understood. Protecting a son who had started rejecting that business and therefore all he stood for, he didn't.'

'So he kicked you out and you didn't even fight?'

'I didn't even fight.' He swallowed back the bile and let the words out. 'Because letting him think badly of me gave me a perfect escape.'

And that was why, where it really counted—in his heart, not his head, he knew he didn't really deserve to be part of a family. He'd deliberately walked away from a second chance. In not paying attention that year, in being too consumed with fighting plans and cutting loose, that group of criminals had deliberately played him and he hadn't even seen it coming.

Needing Amanda, he tugged her over him to hold her close. Soon her breathing evened out and she slipped into sleep. He lay awake worrying; worrying he was going to hurt her, because this living-in-the-moment thing that they were doing, this putting off the inevitable, was so far off a sensible plan, it was crazy. And it smacked of how he had lived his life ten years ago.

Chapter Ten

Amanda smiled softly to herself as she lathered soap across her torso. She had a good mind to call out to Jared and get him to come in here and finish soaping her off. But then he was supposed to be meeting with Nora this morning and if he came in here she was pretty certain one thing would lead to another.

Not that that would be a bad thing, especially if it went down like the night before. When he'd woken her in the night and loved her like there was no tomorrow, not only with his body but with his mind, his spirit, his soul. His heart.

She hummed a little as she switched to rinsing off the bubbles. She was mighty proud of herself. She'd taken that joyful feeling and grasped it hard to her heart.

And it was Jared that had inspired her to do that.

She'd tried to show him that the past may have shaped him, but it didn't mean that that was *all* he was. She wasn't entirely convinced he believed her. He'd been pretty restless in his sleep last night. But if he gave her time, she'd come to make him understand just how loveable he was.

Her breath caught.

Loveable?

As in, loved?

By her?

Her breath rushed out in a strange sort of panicked giggle. And then, because she recognised that what she was feeling really wasn't so scary, she allowed herself to draw another breath.

Of course, this meant a new plan.

Maybe even a 'forever' kind of plan.

She was getting to quite like planning things. Now she laughed in the face of The Planning Gremlins. How was that for progress?

She let herself out of the shower and grabbed the soft fluffy white towel off the heated rail as Jared walked in.

'Hey you,' she said softly, smiling up at him. 'I was just thinking about you.'

'Amanda, I—you're not dressed.'

'I know. I've tried showering with my clothes on, but I like it better this way.'

He didn't smile and her breath hitched because suddenly she knew, without a shadow of a doubt, that somehow the Planning Gremlins had got wind of her daring to have a think about a 'forever' plan and were waiting in the wings for her. And she didn't feel so brave after all.

'I'm putting you on a plane back to New York, tonight.'

She registered his words, registered the deep discomfort in his face, in the way he held himself rigid and apart from her.

Drawing another towel off the rail and wrapping it turban style around her wet hair she asked in as calm a manner as she could muster, 'I thought we weren't leaving until the end of the week?'

'I know. Change of plan.'

'Change of plan?' She looked at him, her head tipping to the side, her eyes narrowing a fraction, 'Why?'

'It's just better this way.'

'Better for whom?'

'Better for us both.' His hand came out of his pocket to run through his hair. He shifted on his feet. 'It doesn't need to become dramatic. I'm simply bringing the arrangement forward by a couple of days.'

Not liking at all how this was sounding she reached for her jar of body cream and began rubbing it over her arms in the hope that the cool lotion would calm her nerves. 'And by "arrangement" you mean..?'

'The plan, then. Your plan. The one where we agreed to go back to being friends after London.'

'Don't you think it will be a little difficult to remain friends if I'm in New York and you're here in London?'

He paused, breathed in and seemed to have difficulty dragging his eyes away from the rhythmic way she was applying the lotion. Turning to study his own reflection in the large mirror, he said quietly, 'My father has asked me to stay on for a while…indefinitely.'

'I should stay here with you. You'll need some support.'

'That's very sweet of you. But I don't need support.'

'I see.' Amanda very carefully put the glass jar of scented cream back on the bathroom counter and turned to meet his eyes in the mirror. 'Don't need it or don't want it?'

He shrugged his shoulders implying she should infer what she wanted and her frustration started building.

He wanted to have this conversation? Fine, but the minute his shutters came down she was going to throw everything she had at him. She crossed her arms and waited until he felt uncomfortable enough to break the silence.

'It's time I learnt how to speak "family" on my own. It wouldn't be right to expect you to wait here indefinitely, putting your plans and your life on hold, for something we both know isn't meant to last.'

Not last. Really? Why not? Minutes ago, under the heat of the shower spray, the two of them making a go of it together had seemed like the most natural, least scary, prospect in the world.

She chewed down on her lower lip. So what he was saying was that last night had been his goodbye. He'd decided. She didn't get a say. Charming.

'Jared, are you just going to pretend last night never happened?'

'Of course not. Last night was incredible. This whole time here with you has been incredible, but like I said, I can't—no, I won't, ask you to give up your dreams and your options, just to stay here with me.'

'You know, last time I checked, these were enlightened times. A woman was allowed to have a lover and a career.'

He picked up her jar, turned it around in his hand. Put it back down on the counter top. 'You forget that I know what it takes to start your own business. The focus it requires. The hours you need to put in. How it starts to consume your every waking breath.' His eyes searched for hers, 'I saw your face when you told me about it. It was like you were lit up from the inside. Fear wasn't even on your radar. That's how excited you were.'

'If you're reducing everything down to black and white,' she breathed in and took her chance, 'What if what I want, what I really want, is to stay here with you?'

There was a brief flare of panic in his eyes before he blinked. 'The people-pleaser in you has you thinking you want to stay here, but it's just not practical. You think because I told you all that stuff last night that I need you but don't know how to tell you? I might not have told any other woman I've been with but that fact doesn't mean what you think it means. I told you because we are friends. Don't try and make it more complicated than that, because you'll get hurt. And I don't want that for you.'

Too late for that, she thought, beginning to shiver.

She needed clothes. Clothes would definitely help her fight. If she could just get warm she would be able to think straight and work out how to make him see and how to make him understand. Spying the bathrobe on the back of the door she brushed passed him, dropped the damp towel and shrugged into the dry robe. She gave it a couple of seconds. It didn't seem to have any effect.

She looked at him from under her lashes. She knew he felt something for her. Knew it. She just had to make him see. 'But Jared—' She heard the plaintive tone. Stopped, licked her lips. She didn't want to be that woman, his Latest Limpet, the one who simply kept whining 'But Jared...' every time he tried telling her "no".

Maybe if she simply told him she loved him? But...how did she do that, then? What if it came out as a pathetic: but I love you? When for him to hear her, really hear her, it needed to be more. So much more. Enough to slip in past those shutters of his and find its way to his heart.

If it wasn't so ironic that it was *her*, standing before *him*, computing all the angles, it would be funny—if only because she was such a novice at it and bound to latch on to anything to make her point.

'Is this about Mikey?' She gambled pathetically. 'You're seeing me in the cold light of day and remembering I'm Mikey's sister?'

'Do you really want to know what Mikey said when I went to your house to confess that you'd kissed me, that I'd kissed you back?'

From the look on his face, she really didn't. But when he continued she found herself rapt.

'He said, "About damn time." Can you believe that? Nobody tells their best friend they think you're perfect for their sister. He kept saying how great it would be to see me happy, see you happy. I tried telling him he was barking up the wrong tree. That you and I were friends. That was all. But he kept on and on. And do you know what? All the time he talked about how he thought we'd be good for each other, it was like I was hearing him from a great distance because all I could think about was that it sounded an awful lot like yet another example of somebody wanting something for me that I didn't want for myself.'

She sucked in a breath. That was low. She'd been preparing to fight for him. It was never going to be easy, but realising he was going to make it as hard as possible for her, hurt. Really hurt.

'Look,' he ground out uncomfortably while she was lost for words, 'I take full responsibility for bypassing the conversation where we worked out how to go back to being friends after this had run its course. And it's selfish of me to need you to understand now. Believe me, you can't make me feel any worse than I already do.'

'I don't want you to feel bad, Jared. I want you to feel—' she broke off as she realised something vital. 'Wait a minute, this *is* about last night. This is about you rejecting me before I get the chance to reject you.'

'It isn't. Men really aren't that complicated.'

'Well, how's this for complicated? I'm in love with you!' she shouted in his face without thinking.

As she watched him stagger backwards, she heard her words echo off the tiles of the bathroom walls and couldn't believe she'd come right out and said it. Mortification arrived bang on cue, because looking at Jared's pale, shocked face, she'd just given him the perfect excuse to call it quits.

When he didn't say anything, merely continued to stare at her, she let the anger rise up to cloak her, 'What, too "vocal" for you? Well, you should have thought about that before you taught me that it was perfectly alright to shout what you wanted from the rooftops. Before you taught me to reach out for what you want; to live life. Not just go through the motions.'

'I don't know what to say.'

He did. He absolutely knew what to say, she thought, breathing hard. 'How about, "I'm in love with you too"?' she pleaded, her voice fading to a whisper because the horror on his face had her heart cracking.

He actually started pacing, like he had to put physical action to illustrate all the work going on behind the scenes in his head as he computed the ramifications of her declaration. It saddened her more than she could ever say.

She realised she had taken courage from thinking he felt the same. Because why on earth would she, Amanda Gray, now distinct hater of going-with-the-flow, lay her cards on the table and laugh in the face of the Planning Gremlins, if she hadn't thought, secretly, deep down that he was in love with her too?

'Amanda, I can't say that back to you.'

'Can't? Or won't?'

He looked thoroughly shell-shocked.

Maybe his brain had forgotten how to work. Maybe he'd forgotten how to go into self-preservation mode.

But then his jaw set solid and she remembered that this was Jared. And with every word he spoke, she saw the shutters coming down. 'If you really believe you are in love with me then New York is truly the best place for you. You'll be near Mikey and you'll have the distraction of the business.'

'You haven't answered my question, Jared,' she said, steeling herself for the battle.

'Damn it Amanda. Don't make me say it. Do you think I want to hurt you? Enough is enough. I don't have time for this. My priority has to be my family.'

Like she would ever ask him to choose! 'You are unbelievable. Are you seriously telling me that in this moment, when I stand here and offer you everything I have to give, you're going to use your family as an exit strategy?'

'I'm telling you please don't offer me anything. I don't deserve it. I'm telling you I'm sorry. This is my fault. I should never have let things get this far. I should have kept reinforcing what I'm like with relationships. But I figured you already knew what I was like in relationships—you've rescued me from enough of them. I fooled myself into thinking we could have each other for a while and it would be fine afterwards.'

'And keeping each other forever isn't an option?' She watched desperately for some sign. 'I'm putting the option right out there for you and you're telling me you don't want it? You see only that you'd have to extricate yourself from someone pushing something on you that you don't want?'

'I'm sorry.'

He couldn't do it. Not even when she'd tried with all her might to lead him there.

The last ray of hope burnt out. 'I'm the one who should be sorry,' she managed, pressing her forearm over her mouth to stop the deep, gut-wrenching sobs that were building up inside of her from escaping. 'It's my bad luck that I seem to have fallen in love with an emotional coward.'

'Amanda.'

'Get out, Jared. Go to your meeting and leave me be for a few hours.'

'I can't leave you like this.'

'I want you to. No, I need you to. If we are to have any shot at remaining friends, I need you to get out of this room right now before I add the fact that you've seen me cry over you to your list of sins.'

She didn't even wait to hear him leaving the apartment before she was peeling off the bathrobe and stumbling back under the needle-stinging shower spray to cry her heart out.

Stupid. She was so stupid to try and fight logic with emotion. So stupid to try and fight his mighty control with untutored influence.

And she was so sorry—so very sorry for laughing in the face of the Planning Gremlins. She hadn't meant to. It wasn't fair. If she could just go back...

By the time she'd cried herself out the water had turned cold. Vigorously towelling herself dry she walked through into her room and grabbed the nearest clean clothes.

On autopilot, with a cool, calm and collected manner she rang the airport and booked herself a ticket on the first plane back to New York. With cold, concise, precision she packed.

And with dry eyes and a gaping hole in her heart, she bid goodbye to London and headed home to heal.

***

'So is Amanda out with Janey tonight?' Jared asked Mikey, when he couldn't handle the suspense and longer.

The two of them were sitting in Mikey's living room, the game playing on the big screen in front of them going largely unwatched as they talked and drank beer.

'No, Janey's with her mother, doing wedding things. Apparently they're sampling sugared almonds. I say, what's to sample? They all taste the same, right, absolutely God-awful.'

Jared took a pull of beer. He had a feeling Mikey was deliberately not answering his question fully in a bid to see how much his friend could take. To be fair, he wasn't sure it would take much to have him rolling over and waving the white flag. Because of that it was probably a good thing that Amanda obviously wasn't at the house, or coming to the house.

Was it because she knew he was visiting for a couple of days before heading back to London? Was he not going to get the chance to see her at all?

He took another pull of beer.

Lord, but he missed her. Physically ached with the missing of her.

The emails weren't enough. But she probably knew that. Had probably worked out that the first one she'd sent three weeks ago, so tentatively asking him how he was, how his family was, had forced him to acknowledge just how much he was missing her.

He'd needed time to assess whether it was appropriate to respond but then a few days later she was sending him another one, reminding him that they'd agreed to be friends, hoping he was still going to come to Mikey's wedding and telling him about the little apartment she'd found, about how she was getting on with her life, starting up the business, still working as a barista part-time.

Without stopping to properly think about the consequences he'd sent her an email back and then immediately after that one he'd sent another, his first attempt at an apology. They had been emailing regularly ever since and yet he hadn't mentioned coming over for a visit in case it scared her away. So where was she? He was too afraid to ask.

It was a sad, sad state in which he found himself. And it was all his own fault. He needed some sort of plan to sort himself out. Recoup.

'Don't worry. Janey's set aside the whole day tomorrow to go through the business with you,' Mikey said, leaning forward slightly to catch a replay on the big screen.

'Better not have another one after this then,' Jared responded holding up his beer bottle.

Mikey shrugged his shoulders. 'How are things with your father?'

'Good. Bad—I don't think it's going to be long now.'

'Figured. You look pretty crap.'

'I guess.' Of course if he wasn't walking around knowing he'd let something precious slip through his fingers maybe he'd look better.

They watched the game in silence for a while.

'Mikey, do you know what Amanda did with the money I sent her?'

'What money?'

'I sent her some extra, along with her wages. Enough to cover start-up costs on her new business.' More than enough, really, and he was curious to know what had become of it, because it sure didn't sound like she was using it in the business if her emails were anything to go by.

'Ah, *that* money. I think she made it into a collage or something like, framed it and used it for a photographic assignment.'

'She withdrew two hundred and fifty *thousand* dollars and made it into a collage?'

'It was pretty huge. That's a lot of money to stick on card. Took her days. Pretty outrageous, huh?'

He stared at Mikey, his mouth open. 'I literally don't know what to say.'

'So I hear.'

His jaw clenched. He'd been wondering when they were going to get down to it. 'Is this the part where you kick me into next year?'

'How about I just take you out the back and shoot you?' Mikey said, turning his chair around until they were facing each other.

It was no less than he deserved, Jared thought. And it might even put him out of his misery. Not that he deserved to be put out of his misery after what he'd given up.

'She told you she loved you, man. Even more impressive and, let me tell you, harder to do, she told you she was *in* love with you and you? You put her on a plane back to New York.'

'Technically she put herself back on a plane.'

'*Technically* you're the biggest horse's arse to walk the face of the earth!'

'*Technically*, can a horse's arse even walk?'

They stared each other down until Mikey appeared to take pity on his friend.

'Do you know what I don't get? I don't get why you won't let yourself be happy? You could be happy with her. She would work every day of her life to make you happy. There's a sort of stubbornness in you, Jared. An unwillingness to compromise, and it ain't pretty. And it's going to have you winding up on your own. And do you know what? Life's too short.'

Amanda walked between the trees at the edge of the lake to take up her position. She'd scouted out the location weeks before and knew exactly where to get the best shots depending on the weather. She smiled. There was just enough cold air coming off the water to lend a mystical quality to the floodlit pagoda beyond. Magic! She bent at the knees and ran off a few shots.

Movement off to the left caught her eye and she lowered the camera. The wedding party had arrived.

She saw Jared before she noticed anyone else and had to swallow hard against the surge of longing.

He stopped and waited with the others as a member of staff from the grounds put a ramp in place for her brother to gain access. She saw him briefly smile at something one of the groom's party was saying, but she'd be willing to bet the smile never quite reached his eyes. Lifting the camera she looked through the lens and adjusted the focus to zoom in on his beautiful face.

Grief had lent an opaque quality to his usually crystal-clear green eyes. The sculpted plains of his face stood even more prominently than usual.

A lump formed in her throat. Her heart ached for him. If she could have reached out across the water and comforted him she would have.

For a moment her attention was taken by the flurries of flower petals being scattered around and she made sure she took a few photographs. It was her job to record everything.

Unbidden, her camera searched him out again.

Now he was standing a little way off from the wedding party, hands in the pockets of his tuxedo. He looked restless and she knew why, *hoped* she knew why.

He was waiting.

For her.

Breathing in to steady her nerves she began the walk that would take her back over the tiny wooden bridge to reach the wedding group. Because she couldn't pass up the opportunity she briefly stopped on the bridge. Rooting around in her bag she picked out a different camera and leant over the side to take a picture of the reflection of the pagoda in the water.

And then she could put it off no longer.

As she walked towards him she forgot about everyone else, only had eyes for him. As if sensing her presence he turned towards her and she could barely breathe.

'Hello, Jared.' She dropped the heavy canvas bag at her feet and smiled tentatively up at him.

'Amanda.' He hesitated, then leant in to press a quick kiss against her cheek but it was too, too fleeting and Amanda wanted to haul him back. 'You look beautiful,' he said, his eyes drifting slowly over

144

the damson velvet evening gown she wore.

'Thank you. It was hard to find something that I could move about in to take photos,' her words drifted to a pitiful end. Great; wasn't she the scintillating conversationalist.

This so wasn't how the conversation had gone in her plan.

She blinked. Just remembering the plan gave her a little boost.

She forced herself to look him in the eye and when she did the plan went out the window. Without even being aware of what she was doing her hand came out to clutch his forearm. 'I'm so sorry about your father.'

'Thank you.'

'I sent flowers.'

'They were beautiful.'

'It wasn't enough.' Oh dear. She could feel the emotion rising up to claim her as she realised that somehow grief had deprived him of the use of his shutters so that he appeared to be completely open to her appraisal.

'Amanda,' Jared stepped forward and took hold of her hand. 'It's alright. *I'm* alright. You don't have to worry. Besides, this is a happy occasion, remember? Your brother's getting married. Later... after all the celebrations, we'll talk. Okay?'

'Okay.'

'Anyway, I think someone's trying to get your attention.'

'What?' she turned to see what Jared was looking at, "Oh. That's Jemima. My assistant.'

'Assistant?'

She was a little embarrassed; a lot proud. 'I realised I really wanted to be able to enjoy the ceremony so I thought about it and organised for her to take some of the photographs for me. She probably has a query on the plan I gave her.'

'Plan, eh? Impressive.'

'There's a lot about me that's impressive, Jared,' she flirted without thinking.

'Oh I've never once doubted the fact.'

145

The look in his eyes sustained her through the ceremony and beyond.

He found her under the stars, sitting on the bridge that spanned the lake, feet dangling over the edge, a camera in her hands, a coat draped haphazardly over her shoulders.

'So how do you think your first professional gig went?' he asked as he sat down beside her and passed her a glass of champagne.

She looked up and smiled. 'You'll have to ask the clients for a proper opinion, but in my opinion? I nailed it.'

They clinked glasses in celebration. 'Are those some of the photographs, there?' he asked, nodding towards the camera she'd been looking at.

'What? Oh. No. These are from something else.'

She didn't seem inclined to share and so he let it go, tried remembering instead, just one of the versions of the conversation he'd rehearsed in his head.

'So it turns out its easier to apologise via email than in person,' he finally ventured.

'Well, duh – everything's easier when you don't have to look into the whites of someone's eyes.'

'I agree. That's why I'm stumbling with my attempt now.'

'Your email was very eloquent. How are you going to top that?'

'I thought I'd try grovelling.'

'Grovelling is good.' Then, confidently, cheekily she asked, 'have you missed me, Jared?'

'More than I will ever admit to,' he answered and was rewarded with her generous and beautiful smile.

'What are your plans for the foreseeable? Are you going to be splitting your time between London and New York?'

'For a while.' His family still needed him for a bit and he was happy to be needed. 'I hear you've been doing some travelling too.'

She wrinkled her nose and took a sip of her drink before answering him.

'Does it feel weird?' she asked, 'To know now that while you were over here visiting with Mikey, I was in London?'

'Well considering I only found out an hour ago... It feels,' he stopped, couldn't not touch her a second longer. Reaching out slowly he tucked a strand of silky hair behind her ear. 'Hopeful.'

She leant in to his touch for the briefest of moments before staring out at the water, seemingly considering his answer. His heart kicked solidly against his chest wall because he had so much he wanted to say to her; needed to say to her.

'So I'm having this little showing of my work tomorrow night, would you like to come?'

He forced himself to mimic the light, uncomplicated tone she was using. 'That depends. Will photographs of my money be all over the place?'

'You heard about that, huh?'

'Mikey thought it was hilarious.'

'It was very cathartic. Wildly spur of the moment. Totally unplanned. Reeked of symbolism.'

For probably the first time in weeks he laughed and the release felt wonderful. 'You are so outrageous.'

'Hold that thought,' she said as she scrambled up, camera in one hand, champagne glass in the other, 'and I'll see you tomorrow, about eight? Wear a suit, with a white button-down shirt.'

'What? Wait.'

Chapter Eleven

Amanda pressed her hand against her midriff in an effort to settle the butterflies. Perched on top of the discreet sales counter at the back of the chic little gallery, she surveyed her work. Everything had gone according to her plan. The tea lights and pillar candles winked up at her from where she'd dotted them around the room. The champagne was cooling in the ice bucket behind the counter; the glasses were polished to a gleaming sparkle. And her photographs were gracing the brick walls, providing the perfect backdrop.

She still couldn't believe that it was her artwork hanging, with perfectly printed tiny white sales stickers underneath. That tomorrow the public would be able to see it, possibly buy it. Madness!

It had been a spontaneous decision to approach the gallery owner with examples of some of her work. It certainly hadn't featured on her five-year business plan. But she'd learnt recently that in order to really live life well you had to balance when to plan and when to seize an opportunity. From an initial, completely nerve-wracking conversation an idea had grown into a collection and then into this showing.

Feeling the silence closing in on her she glanced at her watch. He was late. The butterflies quadrupled.

Maybe he wasn't coming.

Maybe he'd spent all day out-thinking himself in that overly practical, examine-all-the-angles, way of his.

God, what would she do if he didn't come?

No. She was not going to be defeatist. That wasn't the real her. The real her was now optimistic about life.

She hopped off the counter and went out to the back room to root around in her bag for her phone. Locating it right at the bottom, where all phones had a knack of navigating their way to, she fished it out to check for messages.

Maybe she should text him, demand to know where the hell he was, ask him how he could be so dense as to not have understood from all the emails they'd shared over the last couple of months, all the looks they'd given each other at her brother's wedding, the fact that she'd invited him here this evening…that it was all the build-up for A Big Conversation. *The* Conversation. The one where she laid everything on the line—again, now that he'd had time to get used to the idea. Because when he'd sent her that searing apology she'd thought there had been something else behind the words as well; something that had given her hope and allowed her to start planning.

She walked out into the gallery again to check the front door but there was no sign of him. Right. Time for action. She wanted this. It was up to her to get it. Sliding open her phone she texted: **CODE RED, WHERE R U?** and before she could talk herself out of it, hit the send button.

As the minutes ticked by she endeavoured to keep herself busy. Anything to give her some respite from the churning in her stomach and the lump in her throat. She looked down at the remaining pile of printed cards on the sales counter. She squared them up precisely to form a precision stack. Each one read: "Symbols of Hope by Amanda Gray." She smiled…and jumped a mile when her phone buzzed to signal an incoming text. Breathing out she opened the message.

'I'll be there in fifteen, J xx'

Okay. First crisis averted. Of course this meant that he was really coming. In fifteen minutes. To see her. See her exhibition. Hear what she had to say. This was good, right? This was going to work, wasn't it? She was going to risk absolutely everything and open her heart to him. Because she didn't let fear rule her any more, did she? She was fierce! She could do this.

She started pacing. Her mind went blank. She couldn't think of the words. The words she'd been practising in her head for weeks. The words that brilliantly, wonderfully, beautifully, perfectly encapsulated what she felt for him. She racked her brain for all the reasoned, well-thought-out, logical arguments she had composed to illustrate her desire, and paced faster when she came up with a complete blank.

She should have made notes. Dotted flashcards discreetly around the gallery. Worn an ear piece with her words talking quietly in her head. Why on earth hadn't she thought of these things?

By the time she realised she was dangerously close to hyper-ventilating she ordered herself to get a grip.

This was Jared.

Her friend Jared.

Everything was going to be alright. She had faith. She had thought this all through properly.

Glancing at her photographs, she realised that if she got too lost for words she could simply use them to guide her. With a start, she realised she'd left one detail undone and, racing out to the back room, she grabbed up her cream-coloured silk shawl and rushed back out again.

She was just hanging it up over the very last frame when the front doors rattled.

'Just a minute,' she called out, her heart jumping into her mouth.

With one last glance around the room, she ran her shaking hands over her hips to smooth her dress and began the long walk to the front doors of the gallery.

He was standing outside in a midnight-blue suit and snowy,

crisp-white, button-down shirt. It looked freshly starched and she felt her mouth start to water. He was also holding the biggest bunch of flowers she'd ever seen. Oh. Her heart began a slow melt.

She turned the key in the lock and opened the door to him.

'Hi,' she said shyly.

'Hi,' he answered.

'Come on in,' she stood to the side and felt her senses spark into overdrive as he walked through. It wasn't the flowers she responded to but his woody cologne.

'Where is everyone?' he asked.

'Oh. Um, it's just you and me. A private showing.' She licked her lips as her heart thundered in her chest, 'Is that okay?'

He turned to look at her. His pupils expanding, turning the darkest obsidian, almost obscuring the green completely as his gaze travelled over her in her red silk Japanese-style dress. 'It's very okay. These are for you,' he said, presenting her with the flowers.

'Thank you, they're incredibly beautiful.' She took them from him and looked about her in panic. She hadn't thought he might bring her flowers. Where on earth was she going to put them? Maybe Simon, the owner had a vase out the back. She signalled to him to wait in the gallery while she walked towards the back.

'I asked my sisters what type I should get,' he said to her retreating back.

She turned to see him wander over to her first photograph, hands in his pockets.

'Nora said roses, Sephy said lilies. I went with Daisy's suggestion of one of everything they had.'

She smiled, spied a huge glass vase in a twisted pewter frame and plonked some water in it hurriedly before making her way back out to the gallery. When she came out he was standing stock-still in front of the fourth photograph. Nervously she fussed with the flowers. Stroked her fingers over some of the waxy blooms to try and reign in her nerves and then forced herself to walk over to him for his reaction.

'Do you like it?'

'I—,' he frowned and took a tiny step closer, 'Yes.' He said simply. She watched him swallow and looked at the photograph herself, even though she knew every pixel by heart. It was a photograph of a couple holding hands. Their linked hands took up the entire frame so that you couldn't tell who the couple were. She had wanted it like that, just their hands. For her it was one of the strongest symbols in the collection.

'The hands in the picture belong to your parents,' she said softly. 'I took it on my last visit.'

She waited for the shutters to come down and the tiniest sliver of hope unfurled when his face remained open.

'When I was visiting Mikey?'

She nodded. 'When I got back to New York, after some time had passed, I wrote to your father. I felt bad that I hadn't taken the time to say my goodbye. He invited me to visit. He told me he'd like the opportunity to explain some things in person. He apologised for any part he might have played in making his son think he wasn't deserving of love. He didn't have to do that for me, Jared, but he did have to do that for you. I'm glad he was able to tell me he was working hard to form a bond with you before it was too late. I'm glad you and he were given that time, because it's going to help you forge a new place for yourself within your family and its going to give you the peace to heal.'

Jared looked back up at the photograph, 'My father liked you. Not many people in his world had the fortitude to remain themselves around him. He liked how you weren't afraid to show how strong your friendship was with me, how you tried to protect me when you thought I needed protecting. To him it meant I was the type of man who could attract good, honest people into their life. It helped ease the guilt he'd been living with. It was nice to give him that peace at the end. For him to know that his son hadn't become so hard and bitter that he would wind up lonely and alone with no one to share his burdens or successes.' Jared moved on to study the rest of the photographs. He paused over each one; the flower growing out of a crack in the pavement, the circles of light forming a vivid picture of dawn, the pregnant woman with her hand over her belly, the double rainbow, the view from the end of a inky black tunnel, and the picture of an architect's plans for a new office-block complex.

'What about this one at the end here?' he asked, stopping in front of the veiled picture.

'Oh. Well.' She wasn't quite ready for him to see that one yet. 'I haven't quite decided if that one's going to be part of the exhibition,' she answered breathily.

'What's the exhibition called?'

'Symbols of Hope. '

Jared looked around him. 'God, Amanda. I can't help feeling I was right to let you go. Look at what you've achieved.'

Amanda grasped a strong hold of her courage. 'I could have done this anywhere, Jared. *Would* do this anywhere, because it's what I'm meant to be doing with my life. Because this amazing, incredible friend showed me that I have what it takes to reach out for what I want and believe that I'm worthy of it. That same friend had the guts to tell me that if I wanted to control my own destiny I needed a plan and I needed to follow through on that plan regardless of how I feared failure, or feared that it would be taken away from me.'

'Is this the same friend who lost his guts when it counted most?'

She reached out a trembling finger to brush an invisible speck of lint from his shirt. 'I'm thinking he only momentarily misplaced them. I'm thinking, hoping, maybe he's found them now?'

He smiled down into her face. 'I think we might be about to find out. Kiss me for luck?' he said and when she opened her mouth to speak he bent his head to lay his lips gently over hers.

She flung her arms around him and stepped in close so that he couldn't escape. Because it had been too long since their lips had touched and she wanted to drink in all of him. Wanted to rejoice in the pleasure of his lips against hers, wanted to feel his heart pounding beneath his sexy white shirt, wanted to release some of what she was feeling in a way that was more obvious than words she might potentially stumble over.

Before she was ready for his mouth to stop devouring, or for the heat between them to stop flowing, he groaned and broke the kiss. Looking down into her upturned face he ran his fingertips over her cheekbones, smiled and shook his head at himself. 'You are the only woman who has the power to distract me with the slightest of touches. Just one touch is all it takes from you and I'm completely, utterly distracted.' He took a small step away but she didn't want to lose all connection with him and reached for his hand. He looked down at their joined hands and glanced briefly back to the photograph. 'I know you know that I took you to London to distract me from having to face up to meeting my family again. I know you know that and forgive me for it. But I want you to know that my plan backfired on me. In such a short space of time you were no longer the distraction. You were the main focus. And yes, I did start using my family as a distraction from you. And I knew it wasn't right. But I couldn't control the fact that the more I let you in, the more I feared I would end up hurting you.'

'Jared, I came to London with you because it got me out of taking full responsibility for my New Year resolution to focus on a proper, thoughtful plan to kick-start my life. I could tell myself I'd started the plan and then forget about it. I could tell myself I was helping a friend and that took precedence. But I also came to London with you because, deep down I knew you were someone I could test myself with and remain safe with, because you're loyal, honest and true. It never occurred to me that you wouldn't consider yourself all of those things until I saw you with your family.'

'But thanks to you I got to see my family through fresh eyes. Thanks to you I'm able to meet them halfway. I knew I'd made a dreadful mistake the moment I returned to that apartment and found you gone. And when I couldn't stop myself from inventing a reason to fly over for a visit, I had hoped with all my might that you would have been at Mikey's, so that I could have apologised and told you what a mess I knew I'd made of everything. I wanted Mikey to rail at me, beat me, shoot me. Anything to help me feel I was being punished for treating you so callously, so carelessly. But he saw straight through me. Like you, he told me life was too short. And just like that it all clicked into place. In trying to protect your right to have dreams to work towards…in trying to protect you from my fear of repeating old mistakes, I'd forgotten the most important thing, a person's right to choose for themselves. Choice is about control and I took that control away from you and I'm truly sorry for that. I just felt so out of control—have always felt out of control around you.'

'Really?'

'You have no idea. And no idea how much subconsciously I liked that you made me address that control. It made me feel alive. Why do you think I sent so many CODE REDs? Getting to sit opposite you in the Thai Lounge, watching you work your magic, trying to keep a lid on the attraction, telling myself over and over that you were my best friend's little sister and that breaking all these resolutions I had not to touch you wasn't allowed.'

He tugged on her hand and stepped in closer to her. 'It's always been you. You're the one who makes me see the world in a better, brighter way. You're the brave, strong, incredible woman who believed in the man I was in the past and the man I am now, who put both halves together and recognised there was a whole worth having. I'm so sorry I tried to throw all that away.'

'Good job one of us around here knows how to come up with a plan to turn all that around, huh?'

'Did you make a plan for me Amanda?'

'I might have done. Just a little, modest, okay—great big, incredibly complex, thoroughly well-thought-out, backed-up and super backed-up plan to bring you to your senses.'

'Is it weird that I find that incredibly sexy?'

'Well you do like a nice plan!'

'I really do. Have I told you how much I love your outrageousness?'

'I think you just did.'

'Well, it's the truth. Do you know I might have come up with a little plan for you too?'

'You did?'

'I did. Want to hear how it starts?'

'Uh-huh.'

'It starts with me telling you that I love you. That I'm in love with you.' Cupping her chin tenderly with his hand he searched her upturned face. 'How are you liking my plan so far?'

'I'm loving it, I, hang on—wait, this isn't going according to *my* plan. I have this whole speech thing. With props.'

'Props?'

'Well, one prop. A sort of visual aid, really. A kind of, okay… Look, to be honest, the whole telling me you love me thing has made me so happy I can barely breathe, so instead, I want you to hold front and centre in your mind that you love my outrageousness, and, well, why don't you unveil the last photograph and tell me what you think?'

Jared reached up to take the shawl off the picture.

She watched as he stood back to look at it.

She chewed down on her bottom lip. Wrung her hands together and waited.

And when she could not wait any more she took the last step needed to touch his sleeve. 'Well? What do you think?'

'I think it's bold. I think it's brilliant.' He turned towards her, hand in pocket and said, 'And I think, yes. Yes, I will marry you.'

Amanda hadn't realised it was possible to feel so much joy, so much happiness; so much love. They kissed under the photograph of her ultimate symbol of hope: two gold wedding bands nestling on a velvet cushion.

And after a respectful amount of time kissing, Jared eased back, pulled his hand out of his pocket and said, 'This is why I was a little late this evening. I had to stop by your brother's house to collect this.'

'Oh.' Amanda stared down at the blue velvet box, unable to speak. She knew what was inside. The box contained her mother's favourite ring. That Jared had thought to get her brother's permission and that he'd thought about a symbol of continuity. Her heart overflowed.

When Amanda stared up at him with tears in her eyes, he carefully opened the box and slid the ring on her finger. 'I know your parents would be incredibly proud to see all this,' he whispered, indicating the exhibition, 'just as I know they would be incredibly proud of the person you have become. How could they not be? You're beautiful inside and out, Amanda.' Bringing her hand to his lips, he stared down at the ring he had placed on her finger and with pride, bent his head to drop a soft kiss just above the ring. 'You seduced me long before your seduction plan.'

Amanda reached up to lay her hand against Jared's jaw. Because of this man the joyful feeling she had been learning to clasp on to was finally here to stay, making her feel like the luckiest woman on the planet.

Staring up at him and with all the love she had for him shining out of her, she whispered, 'I love you, Jared King. You seduced me into reaching out for life again and I can't think of anything more exciting than making all sorts of plans with you.'

Printed by RR Donnelley at Glasgow, UK